Carter, Mary Arkley
    La maestra. a novel, by Mary Carter.
Boston, Little, Brown [c1973]
    215 p.
    "An Atlantic Monthly Press book."

I. Title.

kf

La Maestra

By Mary Carter

A FORTUNE IN DIMES
THE MINUTES OF THE NIGHT
LA MAESTRA

La Maestra

A Novel by Mary Carter

An *Atlantic Monthly Press* Book
Little, Brown and Company · Boston · Toronto

FIRST EDITION

T 03/73

A portion of "Mimi" is reprinted by permission of Famous Music Corporation.

Library of Congress Cataloging in Publication Data

Carter, Mary Arkley.
    La maestra.

    "An Atlantic Monthly Press book."
    I. Title.
PZ4.C324Ma [PS3553.A7825]   813'.5'4   72-10289
ISBN 0-316-130443

ATLANTIC—LITTLE, BROWN BOOKS
ARE PUBLISHED BY
LITTLE, BROWN AND COMPANY
IN ASSOCIATION WITH
THE ATLANTIC MONTHLY PRESS

Published simultaneously in Canada
by Little, Brown & Company (Canada) Limited

PRINTED IN THE UNITED STATES OF AMERICA

to John

Inasmuch as this is a work of fiction
its characters are fictional.

La Maestra

1 *summer* 1967

It persists, her sensation of being towed. She lies on her back arranged tidily with her arms folded over her chest in the position recommended by the *Red Cross Water Safety Manual*. Her pillow is the lifeguard's shoulder. There is a steady stroking movement under her. The light from the portholes sluices over the cabin ceiling. She lies counting the strokes.

Huh. Huh. *Huh*. HUH. The strokes become audible, approaching in rhythmic thuds down the corridor. Drawing swiftly near they become a runner's thudding footfall; as they pass her door she hears the brush of a runner's terse breathing. HUH. *Huh*. Huh. Huh.

The sound fades off down the passageway and becomes motion once more. She resumes her count of the strokes.

In a cul-de-sac at the end of the Tourist Class dining room five people sit at a round table set for eight. "Vater," a middleaged German woman is saying, "on German ships they serve vine. The Italians are crazy for profit, like the Americans."

"Father Foley's the name," says the tubby little old priest, extending his hand to the woman sitting next to him, "comin back from visitin me nevvew in Newport Beach California." The woman, who is sitting very erect, touches the proffered hand with her own and murmurs, "How do you do." "I didn't catch the name," says Father Foley, putting his hand behind his ear. The woman slowly lifts her gaze. It is gray, the color and sheen of pewter. It locks into his with an invisible click. "I didn't throw it, Father," she murmurs. Then she smiles and the gaze unlocks. "Arabella Sutherland," she says. "Say now, that's a good one," the priest chuckles; "Didn't throw it. Say, have ye heard the one about —"

Also at the table are a huge black Jamaican woman and a dunfaced Italian in an illfitting duncolored suit. Both sit shoveling in immense quantities of food in immense, impassive silence.

"Everyting is crazy in America," the German woman is saying, "the streets are filty and everybody is rude. They let the kids do anyting. They let them run wild. The police have no autority."

"— and the rabbi sez to the bishop, 'That's all foine and well for you,' he sez, 'but it's put three strohks on me golf game.' Hee hee hee hee *sptzz* hee. Three strohks on me golf game. Say, d'ye feel the heat in here, gurl? Lake to rahst us aloive. Makes for a tirrible thirst, tirrible. Lad," he sez to the waiter, "could ye bring us a beer, now. D'ye care to join me in a little beer with yer supper," he sez to the gray-eyed woman. She smiles, shakes her head politely, murmurs to the waiter, *"Chianti, per piacere."*

There is a roar of noisy laughter from an adjoining table, where a group of young American students has been joined by another smaller group.

"This ship is overrun by students and hippies," says the German woman, "in the public lounges there is no place for a respectable person even to sit down. The Americans are afraid of their kids, they gif them cars and money and they run wild, they haf no morals. In Germany they show more respect, they vould not dare —"

"There seems to be no control," the gray-eyed woman says to the Cabin Steward, who has come in answer to her ring, "over the heat in here. It is impossible to sleep, the cabin's so hot." She stands in the middle of her room in a gray silk caftan, her hair falling like a shawl over her shoulders and back. It is brown, with beginning streaks of gray. She is a small woman, erect as a cadet; she levels her pewter gaze at the Steward, smiles politely, and waits.

The Steward, a handsome Italian boy, flicks her a handsome Italian grin. *"La Signora parla italiano molto bene,"* he says. Her smile becomes punctilious. *"Grazie.* My Italian's pretty rusty, I'm afraid. Would you mind checking the thermostat, please?"

The Steward flicks a glance over the thermostat. "It is at seventy-two degrees, Signora. You have been to Italy a while ago, Signora?"

"Twenty years ago. I don't think the thermostat's functioning. The temperature in here is at least eighty-five. I've set it at the lowest point and it doesn't seem to have any effect, it just keeps blowing hot air —"

"Twenty years, *non è possibile,* Signora. Surely the Signora must have been a mere child, a babe in arms —"

"It is not," she says levelly, "a question of my age. I have always loathed overheated rooms."

The Steward meets her gaze. His grin fades. "I will speak with the mechanic, Signora," he says bowing slightly.

She should have left when she saw the movie was *A Man and a Woman.* In this lurching dark the screen seems to emit a different kind of heat, intolerable. Aimée's face, craggy and sensuous, half-hidden by her hair, evokes some dense memory of self, the resemblance between lost conditions. And the man's quick way of glancing at her — that old signal, my God, that click of ardor — explicit as a hand thrust between her thighs.

Rupturing this second maidenhood, this widowhood.

To be loved (she wrote once, long ago when she was beginning her journal) *is to be drowned. The sensations are the same: the flash review of one's history, the sinking into a fathomless embrace, the penetration by a liquid element, and the conviction that this — for the final time — is it.*

"*È Italiano?*" A scragglebearded kid, stretched out next to her in the row of deckchairs by the pool, has nipped in with a match to light her cigarette. "American. Thank you," she says. She lies back again, raises her face to the sun, closes her eyes.

"You on vacation?"

"No."

"You, uh, live in Italy or something?"

"I'm going to be teaching there this year." She turns her face, eyes still closed, away from him.

"Teaching, that's great. You, uh, what do you teach?"

"Political History."

"Political History, that's great. Where?" When she does not appear to hear him he says, "I mean where in the United States, what college?"

"Berkeley."

"Berkeley, that's great. How's the, uh, scene at Berkeley? I mean I'm at Columbia myself, I hear the Movement's died down some there, at Berkeley I mean, I'm in Art History myself but a lotta the people I know are into the —"

"The scene's pretty much the same everywhere nowadays, I guess." She sits up, squashes out her cigarette on the deck, stands. She is wearing a black bikini. "Excuse me," she mutters, "I'm going to cool off." She stalks over to the pool and dives in tidily.

Huh. Huh. *Huh*. HUH. She awakens in the night to the runner's approaching footfalls in the passageway. She has been dreaming; she awakens gasping with the runner's pants that seem to come from her own lungs. HUH. *Huh*. Huh. Huh. The footfalls fade but her chest struggles as if the weight of the body in her dream were still riding her. He was never that heavy. She lurches from her bunk trailing the dream from her naked shoulders like drenched blankets.

You aren't him. She stumbles about her cabin clasping her pillow and striving against its softness to break through to the hardmuscled chest of the dead man. *You were never that heavy,* she grunts, grappling; *at the last there was hardly anything left of you at all.* Six months of halflife days it took and each day diminished him by half his essence. Now after six more months of halflife days her own essence is exhausted. She climbs back onto her berth and rearranges herself in the proper position. Resumes the act of will: lets herself be towed.

They have entered a grayness which seems to suspend them between layers of the same watery element. The ship is massively steady. The sense of motion becomes static, manifest in the shiver of water in the glasses, the shudder of liquid in the inner ear.

It is the night of the Captain's Gala. A bottle of champagne at every table. "It is an American champagne," the German woman is saying; "do they tink ve do not know that the American grapes are inferior to the European? Do they belief that a single bottle is sufficient for five persons?"

"Niver moind, it's enough to sour the milk with," sez Father Foley, popping the cork. "Milk, oof. Come now gurl, drink up, we can order us another bottle. Say, did ye hear the one about the rabbi and the leprechaun? It saymes the rabbi was visitin his auld Irish aunt —"

"Dey tink vith a liddle vine dey can get avay vith slow serviss," the German woman says presently, "by de time he vill bring usss the zooop it vill be cold —"

In the Ballroom the colored lights rotate wildly over the throng of kids rotating wildly to the beat of the Italian band beating out old twist rhythms. Trying to edge around the outskirts on her way to the Library, Arabella feels a hand grab her wrist and some kid pulls her in; she's caught up in the gyrating mass of young bodies so she writhes along awhile working her way over to the doors; disengages herself and panting, heads for the outside air.

Out on deck it's steamy as an orchid house. Pairs of dark figures clot the rail. She passes them with lowered head; the sound of her heels ruptures their intimacy in the throbbing, intimate stillness. She stops at the stern and lights a cigarette; leans her elbows on the rail. There is a vaporous refraction rising from the moonpath. The sleeve of her dress clings to her arm. Her clothes cling layer upon thin layer to her body. Music drifts down from the First Class deck, where a couple standing at the rail casts a single long aureoled shadow, a dark beacon in the white mist.

A man slowly passes, stops at the rail a bit beyond her, stands pondering down at the wash. She can feel his wary attention. She is seized with a desire to laugh: it is such a movie set. She flicks her cigarette away but misses her aim and it bounces off the rail and falls at her feet. She grinds it under her heel and turns away. The man pivots on his elbow, watching her cagily. As she passes she looks into his face. It is bearded; but above the beard the eyes are so young, so greedy, she feels as if she had unwittingly trapped a little ferret cub in the shrubbery where his mama stashed him. Wanting to reassure him she hesitates; he sees this and his face glazes with irresolution and then panic. She turns her back on him and immediately moves away, fiercely swallowing the pity for them both that had formed like a stone on her tongue.

Toward the end of the evening she closes her book and departs the Library. On her way to her cabin she crosses the Lounge, which is deserted now; only the music piped in from the Ballroom and the German woman sitting alone on a leatherette sofa, dressed in her ballgown of lilac rayon.

Arabella hesitates; then she sits down beside the German woman. "I understand," she begins rapidly because of the strange weight on her tongue, "it's not easy. It's hard, being left with ashes on your hands. No matter that it's not you who personally lit the fire; no matter that what you mourn is not the loss of love but the loss of power." The words sound babbled, rushing around the stone. "I think that power, like love, must have a feel of *rightness* about it, so that we who are possessed of it feel that *we* are right. And so losing it, we have the feeling that somehow we may have been wrong; and thus we feel wronged. I want you to know," she finishes, hurrying because she understands it is far too late, "that I realize it can't be *easy.*"

The German woman looks up — dressed in her lilac finery which is the sheen and color of despair, the hue of anteroom walls — and the German woman draws back her lips and the skin around her eyes in a grin, so that under the tight skin the shape of her skullbones emerges. And down over the skullbones trickle dry, slow tears, for the grin has become her way of weeping. Arabella lays her palm alongside the cheekbone of the woman's face. The woman weeps silently, dryly, without a sound. Then she stops. She pulls away, rises stiffly, and stumps out of the Lounge. Arabella looks at her palm, wet with the woman's tears. Sitting erect on the couch she tidily folds her palm into her lap. From the Ballroom the music drifts in.

> . . . *good night, ladies,*
> *good night, ladies,*
> *we're going to leave you now.*

Back in her cabin, she slips her dress off over her head, slips off her slithery silk stockings, slithers out of her slip and into her gray silk robe. Slips into her berth and arranges herself in the proper position: ulnae crossed chastely over the breastbone, femur and tibiae lined up straight and parallel, ossicles floating in the shivery liquid deep inside her skull. Lies here waiting, counting the strokes. Huh. Huh. *Huh.* HUH.

2 *summer* 1967

Halfway up the palazzo staircase I pause to wait for the portiere. His breath rattles in his chest as he toils up the dim stone well, my trunk on his back. As he lurches past he shoots me a glance of operatic agony. I remember that look. Twenty years dissolve.

I hasten up the last two flights. I pause, blinking, in the dusk of the landing lit by a single bulb. Then step forward to press the doorbell under a little brass plaque engraved with the name BRUNELLI.

The table is a long tundra populated with thinly scattered little colonies. Here at the approaches, the Brunelli heir and me; out in the midlands, facing each other with an impression of enemy camps, a shaggyheaded youth and a fat girl with a bulldog countenance; and down at the hinterland reaches, the old Signori Brunelli, grazing through a pile of breadsticks lying between them. Between these outposts a plump maid shuffles supplies: steaming bowls of minestrone, spaghetti, chianti . . .

"Nyazz," roars Ugo Brunelli. "Se-ven years of La-tin I have studied. Six years of Math-e-matics." He plants his elbows on the table and bends back his thick fingers one by one. "Twelve years of His-to-ry."

History hangs heavy on this Brunelli. He sweats heavily. His heavy nose supports the heavy frames and thick glass of his spectacles. His voice thickens the evening heat, it is so heavy; the effect is all arhythmic confusion, like a storm at sea. Middle age hangs heavily on the thick column of his torso; scholarship sits heavy on his brow. He holds (he tells me) two doctorates, Civil Law and Art History, and a position — clerk — in the city offices at Palazzo Vecchio. His pompadour is thick, heavy, immaculately oiled. He wears a lavender shirt with the monogram *B* embroidered on the pocket. He was born (he is saying) in this palazzo, in these very apartments, in the very room and bed which I am to occupy. All (I gather) is exactly as it was at the moment of the Nativity. Everything remains here monumentally Historic.

Noted for my journal:

The genealogy of the Brunelli traces the rise of Florence itself. Traders, merchants, moneylenders, politicians, one branch of the family was connected to the Albizzi, another to the Cerchi; it was said that the Brunelli women — one of whom bore Clement VII two bastard daughters who died in the plague — were great beauties. In the last century the Brunelli were architects, doctors, and attorneys, and still commanded respect as far abroad as Siena.

I plunge the heavy fork into the spaghetti, hoist. My wrist buckles. How could I have forgotten the crushing Florentine heat? Why — at eight in the evening of a day which has baked its way through these thick palazzo walls — are the windows closed to the outside air? Somewhere there is a heraldic roll of thunder.

"Nyazz," thunders Brunelli, mopping at his face with his napkin, "my grand-fa-ther was a pro-fes-sor of me-di-cine. My fa-ther is an ad-vo-cate —"

"Ee-tally-anno." Cutting across the roll of Ugo's voice, the heraldic blare of an English trumpet. *"Pare-kay non parly-ammo ee-tally-anno?"* The grazing heads lift. "Few don't mind, Ugo," continues the fat girl with a pugilistic push of the lower lip, "that was the arrangement. Only Italian spoken at the supper table. I s'pose," and she rolls a popeyed stare down the table at me, *"you* don't speak Italian either?"

I meet the child's gaze. It is avid, starved; it leans into me as if into a wind. "I've probably forgotten most of it," I mumble. "It's been twenty years."

"Ought to keep things *up,"* snaps the child. She is probably fifteen. She looks like Winston Churchill in drag. It is clear in her bullying, starved stare that she knows this. "I s'pose we'll have to make do with wretched infinitive forms. We ought to introduce ourselves, since Ugo hasn't seen fit to. I am Mavis Wedge." She rolls her bowling-ball stare across at the shaggyheaded youth, who has emitted a short barking sound into his spaghetti. "And *that* is Langer Greene. American, of course. Can't speak a word, not one word, of Italian. And he's been here a month."

"A week." I get a glimpse of the kid's face before it

shovels back into the spaghetti. It is wry, cagey, Jewish, with the unmistakable glaze of the American who speaks only American and always will.

"*Two* weeks actually," Mavis barks to the top of the shaggy head; "and one can learn, Langer, if one pays *attention.* *Pare-kay è venuta a Firenze?*" The switch to Italian is thunderous, as if the force of her voice could ram understanding into me the way a hurricane can ram a straw through a plank.

Battered by these linguistic storms, by the heat, by sheer arrival, I gaze helplessly at the child. Her fat face flushes; there is the sense of her planting herself more firmly against the wind. "I say you *are* rusty. I asked why you came to Florence. I mean what do you intend to *do* here?"

I murmur that I intend to teach, and she says teach what; I say I shall be lecturing on Political History, and she wants to know where; I say at the University, and she says do I mean the *Università per Stranieri;* and while I am trying to remember, "Nyazz," Ugo explodes, "you are then a professor?"; and I must have nodded because he bellows to the old Signori out in the hinterlands *"È professoressa all'università,"* and there is a far, startled nodding of white heads and bleats of *Professoressa, da vero, sens'altro, bravissima,* and Ugo with a heavy hand splashes more wine in my glass and begins once more to recount the history of his own scholarship "— six years of Eng-lish; four years of German —" when Mavis thunders jealously *"Parly-ammo ee-tally-anno all tavola"* and then it seems at last to be over. Night has arrived. The old Signori have risen.

We rise, remain at attention while the elders come toiling

past us, each leaning on a cane and the other's arm. The old
Signore, half his wife's size and dapper as a groom-doll on a
wedding cake, bows to me as he taps past, popping his knees
in a tiny curtsy. The old Signora inclines her head, murmuring her *buona notte* in a voice like a groan, managing to
convey with a shrug that such a small formality is a travesty
on what would have been possible in earlier, healthier, infinitely snazzier days. She must once have been imposing;
now she is doubled over with arthritis. They totter their way
out of the *sala* and down some dark corridor, from which
presently issue sharp yips, a skirmish of feeble commands —
Domi! Cita! Eeeh Dio — and a skitter of claws as a small
black poodle hurtles into the room. "Aew," squeals Mavis,
"here's the little lamb wanting its nightly bikkie," and
lunges toward the poodle but Ugo has already scooped it up
and there follows what seems to be a savage struggle for the
poodle's favor. As the shaggy youth sidles past he catches
my eye in a brief countryman's flick and slopes away. I follow him blindly, lose him in a maze of dark hallways until
at last I see a crack of light; opening the door I find myself
in what seems to be a pantry, where the old Signori and a
very tiny entirely cubic old lady sit at a table bathed in the
single blue light of an enormous TV; they glance up startled,
the square little old lady throws up her hands and her apron
and scuttles over to me scandalized squawking *Eeeeh la
Signora professoressa,* and shocked apologies and something
about my *camera,* to which she leads me at last.

An-tooooo-nio . . .
A morning voice, sleepy and plaintive, floating down into

some hollow. Trailing sheets I stumble to the tall window, draw the white curtain back over my naked shoulder, blink out at the plane of golden light: tall wall of tawny stone rising out of the dim square hollow of the cortile below. *Buon giorno, Signora.* Leaning out of a little window cut in the stone, the Brunelli maid sends across her lazy greeting. And rising less lazily up from four tall flights down in the court: a sharp wolf whistle. My naked shoulder and I retreat behind the curtain.

Shortly, a rap on the door and the maid, Lina, comes bearing coffee, bread, apologies. Antonio the porter wishes to convey to the Signora his profound regrets for his son's impudence; no rudeness was intended to the Signora, whom the boy mistook — from down in the dimness of the cortile — for a young girl; it was a natural error and the Signora will understand that boys will be boys . . . etc. etc.

And Italians will be Italians. I grin at Lina and tell her to assure Antonio there's no offense. And so I have, indeed, awakened this morning back in Italy.

I sit in the bathtub under the parsimonious trickle, dun-colored like the trickle (I remember) of the Arno. Lina the maid comes in, feigns apology, makes motions of cleaning the bidet. Lina is a big plump amiable matron with a handsome face and fine moustache. She moves majestically, like the *Queen Mary,* swirling the rag limply around the bidet and telling me about her nineteen-year-old daughter who works as a *venditrice* in a boutique on via Tornabuoni. She wipes her hands on her black rayon skirt and shows me a snapshot. The daughter is very thin and chic and has the no-nonsense stare of the *fiorentina*. I recall that stare: twenty years ago it would not have been chic, but starving. I compliment Lina and ask if her daughter is married. Lina says no, she wishes a career as a model. And besides, she giggles archly, she, Lina, does not wish to be a grandmother yet; she is too young, she says, only thirty-four. I compliment her. Lina's face is indeed smooth and young (a fat pad under the skin tends to prevent wrinkling). She protests: surely she is much older than the Signora? I say that on the contrary I am almost six years older than she. "But you are so thin, Signora, the body of a girl." She says nothing of my face, which has its edges. I say nothing of her body, which does not. We smile at each other. She ambles out, leaving a fine gritty deposit of cleanser in the bidet.

I unpack my trunk. *"Mamma mia,"* gasps Lina, *"è biblioteca!"* She is scandalized to find I have brought not a lady's wardrobe but a veritable library. Panting, on her knees, she hauls out books, manuscripts, ledgers, texts, papers, notes, boxes of file cards — "I'll take that," I say, relieving her of my blue-bound journal; it is the very heart, the central organ, of my work, of — I suddenly perceive, seeing it now reappear in alien hands, in this alien country — what I have somewhere in this travel between come to think of as my life. "I'll take care of the rest," I say to Lina, dismissing her.

I arrange my desk. Typewriter here, references there, notes stacked tidily in this drawer, manuscripts in that, file cards in their file of boxes. *The Rise and Fall of Sociopolitical*

Systems: A Comparative Study of Precocity and Senility.
What a movie it would make.

I arrange my desk. I arrange my body, upright and expectant in its chair, knees together, feet planted firmly, elbows in, fingers poised. I arrange my mind: whisk out bits of lint, flick the switch of the air-conditioner, punch the buttons programming the synapses for the Question:

The Question is

. . . What?

The Question, the Question here we are getting back to

. . . Where? What: where?

The Question, it is a Question of, Oh God a Question

. . . of something, of anything; write anything, it will come, the thing is not to panic, the Question will arrive.

By evening of the first day I have managed to sweep up a neat little pile of lint:

Ugo gets up at 6:30 a.m., has a cup of coffee in the kitchen with old Agata the cook and walks to Palazzo Vecchio where he works from 8 until 2 p.m. He eats a leftover lunch alone at the long sala table watched by Domi the elderly little poodle. Then he and Domi stroll to piazza Repubblica where (Lina says) he browses through the newspapers over a glass of vermouth and examines the shop windows. At 6 he returns to help his mother to the English Tea Room, where she sips aperitifs with her dowager pals until 7, when Ugo comes to walk her home, she dressed in furs despite the heat and leaning heavily on his arm. He and Antonio the porter carry her up the palazzo stairs and Ugo retires to his room until the 8 o'clock meal. After, he goes out to play cards in his neighborhood bar. He doesn't return until midnight, sometimes later. Last night I awoke and heard him out on the terrace saying, "Fai pipi, Domi. Fai pipi, carino."

È andata fuori oggi, Signora? The old Brunellis know very well I've not been out today nor any of the six days since I arrived. *Fa troppo caldo,* I say: too hot. They roll their eye-balls; whoever heard of an American with a sane attitude toward the Florentine climate?

We lunch alone, the old Signori and I. Langer has begun classes at St. John's Episcopal Country Day School and is away until four. Mavis's activities are mysterious. She some-times appears and sometimes does not; she hints at "appoint-ments," which she makes to sound sometimes like romantic trysts and sometimes like cell meetings. I don't press her. The child is starved for drama.

"It's quite obvious, y'know," she said to me last night after dinner, following me to my door. "What's obvious, Mavis?" "Why you stay holed up in your room." I paused with my hand on the knob. "Well, as I'm neither a mad dog nor an Englishman —" "Oh it's not so much the heat," she snorted, "as the timidity. Heh. Heh-heh." "And just what," I said, "am I timid of?" "You're s'posed to be a scholar. Scholars are terrified of learning anything new. Might inter-fere with their neat little theories," she said triumphantly, "might block the flow of logic. Take Ugo, f'rinstance. Degree in Art History and d'you know the last time he was in the Uffizi? Thirty years ago when he went with his class. *That's* a scholar for you. Thirty years, and the Uffizi just around the corner."

After lunch, lying in my darkened room like an ocean bottom under fathoms of heat, sunk in a hallucinatory coma wherein tongues of color flicker behind the eyeballs and images stir an old, fitful lust, pinned flat by a weight — of food, of wine; surely of that huge meal? — I hear myself groaning a name. I start up; the weight moves off me, back into a corner of the room where it coagulates into a watchful shadow. Who is watching?

Not him: I laid the coins over his eyes; I sealed his ghost inside his skull. Why do I fear to unseal myself from these rooms and after twenty years go back out into this old city?

The Question is sealed inside my head. Blocked; I must unlock the old block.

Find the key. Think: when did I use it last? When was the Question last locked in, when was it last that my work froze, history stopped . . .

I laid the coins over his eyes and history stopped. It stopped — I grin grimly, remembering — for a week (they told me) after which the lock was so thoroughly lubricated the key turned easily and there was the Question nice and shiny and bright as new and I went briskly back to my work. How wonderful Arabella was (they told me), able to get back to her work so soon.

I ring for Lina.

Fegato. That is the diagnosis of old Agata the cook as she stumps into my room trundling what sounds like an iron drum full of glass shards which she thrusts under my nose and commands me, Drink. The tautology of the day, considering how it's been spent. I raise the old wrecking ball from the pillow and I obey. There is a small explosion as the remaining wall of the palazzo collapses. Agata removes the glass, picks up the empty bottles, and sets them on the tray where they rattle about in her palsied grasp. *"Meglio?"* she demands. I nod feebly. If not better, no wiser.

At eighty-three, Agata would know better than to lose her Question. She's been tending the Brunelli household for over a quarter-century. She was once — Lina is my informant — a member of a rich Florentine family of jewelers who owned a palazzo around the corner on Borgo San Jacopo. They suffered terrible reverses in the War and during the retreat of the German occupation troops Agata's husband and two sons were blown up with the palazzo, where they'd been harboring Resistance members. Agata had at the moment of the disaster been taking a glass of tea with her old school chum Signora Brunelli. With no place to go, she stayed on as cook. Agata lives in the kitchen and the little windowless room which was once a pantry, her only possession a giant TV. She eats alone and she addresses her old friend as *Signora:* caste is the last thing the Florentine will surrender.

She steadies the bottles with her other palsied hand. "The weather," she announces, "will soon turn cooler. Then perhaps the Signora will go out?"

"Perhaps."

"The autumn is pleasant in Florence. But of course the Signora knows this, having been in Florence before?"

She waits for affirmation; I nod. "When?" demands Agata relentlessly. Just after the last war, I say.

"But of course it is all changed now. It is restored. Everything," Agata continues relentlessly, "is as it always was. Florence is once again a wealthy and beautiful city. The economy is very healthy. People are no longer poor —"

And your pantry is again a palazzo? She has paused (surely I didn't say that last aloud?); she shifts her weight to the other foot, resteadies the bottles. "I understand the Signora is a scholar of history?" I wince; nod. "I understand the Signora is writing a history text?" "Not," I mutter, "at the moment." She ignores the edge of whimper. "Florence is a very historic city," she says fiercely, "so of course the Signora, as a historian, will wish to see with her own eyes that its glories have been completely restored, and that it has reassumed its important place in the world." And she stumps out, empty bottles vibrato on the tray.

So even irresistible history has its Resistance, its fierce little pockets of holdouts. I turn my unpinned coward's face into the pillow. Times are when funk is muck enough, spunk makes it unmuckable.

The palazzo gates swing open. The porter bows me out. I draw a breath; then strictly business stepping briskly out I march down via Maggio across the bridge into piazza Trinità peel off a right and a left and out into piazza Repubblica. As ugly a square as I remember. Then straight across briskly dodging Fiats — oops — hard right and there it is: old Duomo. Bellybutton of history, struck by a sword of light like some civic angel of Annunciation. Once briskly around, steady as she goes. Then home. The porter bows and the gates swing closed.

"All this time you have been here?" The Director of the Cultural Exchange Program is visibly offended. He had ex-

pected to be notified of my arrival. Twice he had planned
— and then been forced to cancel, Signora — a *ricevimento*
in my honor. Only yesterday, he informs me stiffly, he had
under the pressure of anxiety gone to the personal expense
of cabling Berkeley to determine my whereabouts. The
students have arrived. The program will commence in a
little over a week. He, Carlo Ferini, had personally planned
to devote himself to the Signora's orientation. The Consulate
had been telephoning to inquire about the small, intimate
banquet they give each year for visiting academics and
artists . . .

I say I have been working. Ah? he says haughtily. On my
book, I say. "Ah," he says. He invites me to tea.

Younger than I expected, Carlo Ferini is otherwise — from
the tone of his letters — expectable: the very model of the
modern neoactivist, arrogant with humanistic virtue, po-
lemic, priest-eating, possessed of the classic anguish of the
neointellectualist — a passion for scholarship and as passion-
ate a contempt for academe. Ferini is a beautiful lightboned
man with a beautiful lightboned apricot-skinned American
Negro wife. A triumphant ploy, matters of true love aside:
how better for the basically arch-conservative Florentine to
correct the curse of privilege?

Cassandra silently pours tea from a magnificent antique
silver pot into chipped UPIM mugs, while Carlo — in a
bravura display of pyrotechnic Italian laced with some
exquisite American profanity — manages to shoot down the
usual pigeons (Racism, Suppression, Exploitation, Milita-
rism, Imperialism, Neo-Fascism, the Protestant Ethic, etc.)
and in passing to wing or cripple Philosophy, Modern Art,

Theology, Literature, Science, Technology, the new African states, Apartheid, American mothers and cuisine and cars and film and wine — and the rules of soccer, which he claims are flawed and thus basically antithetical to its philosophy.

He manages this sitting edgily at the brink of his elegant Florentine chair crossing and recrossing his elegant legs and following with adoring eyes and nervous shouts — *"Fai cauto, Marco! Cassandra, perchè non lo guardi?"* — the movements of their son, a stunning two-year-old with skin and hair the color of creamed apricots who lunges about the room somehow managing to avoid disembowelment, lobotomy, and third-degree scalds. Cassandra's face is touched with what seems to be pity for something she does not comprehend, and is so beautiful it is hard to see into it clearly. She sits silently watching the baby and disappears a great many times into the kitchen to return bearing dozens of tiny sweet pastries of which nobody but the baby could eat more than two.

"Do anything you wish with your seminars," Carlo instructs as I rise to go. "You will find the quality of students inferior to that of your graduate scholars at Berkeley. Most of these exchange kids are spoiled little bourgeois shitasses from elitist schools which *naturalmente* are uncontaminated with any tinge of the Movement" — he gives me a complimentary nod, for Berkeley — "and which seem to be what the American establishment deems safe to ship us. We get one or two who keep their sphincters open but the rest could use a firecracker up their asses, which I understand that you, Signora, know how to apply." I murmur something about the only real firecracker is objectivity but he ignores it, obviously having decided that any Political Historian from Berkeley has got to be a proper flaming nihilist; he sees me to the apartment door. Unbolts the four locks protecting them. Bows formally and in the prescribed manner murmurs *"Arrivederlà, Signora."*

Pretending to take a break from my "work" each afternoon I sit in a corner of a cool little tearoom around the corner on Borgo San Jacopo, order a *capuccino,* peruse the evening edition of the Florence newspaper *Nazione.* The mayor has ordered another "study" of the appalling traffic conditions clogging the center city; the shopkeepers are shouting *fascisto,* trying to cut free circulation and enterprise; the taxi drivers are threatening another *sciopero,* a strike for Freedom, Bread, the People (who knows where the key may fit, unlocking the Question?).

Looking up to order another *capuccino* I snag not the waiter's eye but Mavis's. She is hunched at a table in the other corner, schlupping the remains of an enormous tea. Trapped with cakecrumbs up to her elbows she freezes; there is the stripped bleakness of starvation before the gaze closes under the bullying scowl. "Thought you were working," she snarls.

"Even scholars take breaks." I smile.

The scowl deepens. "I don't s'pose you'd care for a cup of tea." I hesitate. "My treat," she snarls. "Oh, you don't *have* to of course. No obligation. None."

"In that case I accept."

"In the least. Was simply offering. You probably detest tea. Most Americans — Beg pardon?"

"I said I accept."

"I *say*." She sits stunned, then lurches up; with a great snapping of fingers and bawling of orders — *Cameriere* — and sloshings-over of teapots and cakeplates she settles in cozily, hungrily, schlupping away while I sip gingerly at my tea, which I detest.

Mavis (it seems) considers herself a Remittance Man, although she could have gone back to Ireland with her parents on this leave. Mavis's father is rector of the Anglican church, across via Maggio in what used to be Machiavelli's stables — which, if you ask *her,* still stink of manure. Mavis detests Italy. They dragged her here, kicking and screaming, when she was nine. She didn't want to leave Ireland — *northern* Ireland, she says, the Protestant part — as she had already decided that her destiny was to remain and fight the dirty Catholics and their filthy Persecution. She has found that Italy is the very seat of Catholic Persecution, which she is remaining to study for another five years, after which she will return to Ireland and run for Parliament.

"Oh, laugh if you like," she says fiercely (I have not been laughing); "someday, despite everything, I shall make my mark."

"I believe you."

"I rather thought you would. One sees it in your face," she says crisply. "Although aside from that there's no similarity. None. Heh. Heh-heh." She laughs bitterly. "Too bloody bad for *me,* isn't it."

"Aside from what?"

"The determination to make one's *mark*. It's on your face. Despite the fact you're a woman. Women's faces are their destiny, y'know. Theory of mine. Take my case. My face is quite impossible, of course. People can't take one seriously, face like this. You probably never noticed, not needing to naturally, that *men* can be bloody ugly without being ludicrous but women can't."

"Oh come now —"

"Don't," she snaps. "Don't tell me I'm not ugly. Frankly I hadn't put you down for that kind."

"What kind?"

"The kind that corrupts the young by pretending not to grasp an unpleasant truth." She sloshes the last of the tea into her cup, pours in sugar. "So naturally one simply has to *transcend*."

"How?"

"I haven't the foggiest." She raises her gaze bleakly. "I don't s'pose you've got any suggestions? And don't tell me to be *nicer*. People start liking you and then they pity you, can't have any *authority* with people going about pitying you. Much better to be hated; much. Or feared. One could become a barrister — they're feared, y'know, because they're tricky, know the ins and outs. Only trouble is, one's still a woman. Take an ugly man who's a barrister. They say Oh, what an ugly barrister. Take an ugly woman who's a barrister, they say Oh, what an ugly woman. You see the theory?"

"Yes."

"Rubbish. How could you? Look at you. You think you have authority as a *person* but it's really your authority as a *woman*. I doubt you're even aware of the difference. I s'pect you're trying to be kind. If we're going to be chums, you'll have to be honest. Kindness tends eventually to corrupt," she says bleakly. "Breaks down the moral fibers."

Meanwhile (Mavis resumes) she is pondering ways to break down Persecution — "Y'know where they're excavating under the floor of the Duomo? One could plant a bomb down in there" — and playing hookey every afternoon from the Italian public school — "Ridiculous. Medieval. They encourage the girls to take sewing and the boys get to take Algebra," and hanging around the Ponte Vecchio, observing "those filthy hippies, who talk about Activism but never *do* anything. Of course not one will ever make his *mark*."

Huh. *Huh*. HUH. *Huh*. Huh.

Returning across the Ponte Vecchio of a sodden heat-heavy late afternoon, as the Florentines reemerge from the siesta, I turn from the antique-shop window but it is too late: the runner has passed, his wake a closing swath of indignant Florentines, an elegant lady clutching her poodle, an old gent brandishing his stick, cries of *pazzo!* Madman indeed, running in this heat. *Craaaaaazy,* murmurs an American hippie to his chick as they recline with the backs of their necks propped against the bust of Cellini.

I scurry on across but the *piazzetta* is a tangle of traffic so I turn up Borgo San Jacopo — head him off at the pass — and pick up a few angry looks myself, jostling clots of strollers, these slow everlasting inspectors of their city's minutiae, my God, this race of street people . . .

No way. I turn into the tearoom and seek out my quiet

corner where with my back to the wall I won't get ambushed.

Coming through the palazzo gates in the twilight, I see Langer Greene dismounting from a Vespa, leaning it carefully against one of the cortile pillars. Antonio the porter, who has been lolling at the portals lipping a toothpick and surveying the evening traffic jam, decides it is time for a little Italian flap. He shuffles up to Langer, waving his arms and speaking excitedly. Langer blinks at him from under the crash helmet. "What's he saying?" Langer says to me. "He says you can't park your cycle in the cortile," I explain. "How come?" Langer wants to know. Antonio waves his arms and his voice. "He says it is not allowed to park vehicles in the cortile." "So how come there's this Fiat always parked in here," says Langer. I translate; Antonio begins clutching at his shirtpockets. "He says the Fiat is his son's and is used to conduct the business of the palazzo. He says any violation of the parking rules will cause the Barone to fire him, Antonio, and throw his poor little family out on the street." "Jesus," mutters Langer, "who's this Barone?" The Barone, it seems, owns the palazzo and is the brother-in-law of the mayor. It seems also (I draw Antonio aside to determine this) that the parking rules can be stretched a bit, as a personal favor from Antonio, who will intercede with the Barone in the name of Reason, Justice, and Italian-American relations, for a very small gratuity, say five hundred lire daily. "Why didn't he just say there's a parking fee?" mutters Langer, forking over his eighty cents.

Langer (he says, lolling on my sofa while we're waiting for the dinner call) spent the summer on an Israeli kibbutz tying up grapevines. Israel sort of turned him on, he says. He claims to have been able to detect the Israel–Arab border. "There was like all this green," he says, "like you know, fields and orchards. And then" — slicing motion — "nothing. Desert. Rockheap. Wilderness."

"No burning bushes?" I grin. "Pillars of fire?"

"Yeah yeah yeah." He grins back, unruffled. "That's for the orthodox." A new kind of orthodoxy, this tribe of Langer's — blue-eyed, evolved — underwrites the Promised Land; his kind of Jewishness holds the mortgage now. Every vine and grapefruit and blade of miracle alfalfa springs from their money, the bourgeois magnates', poured in to irrigate the holy soil and repossess the myth. Out of neohumanism, the old fierce warrior tribe is reborn. Langer arrived in Israel just after the Six-Day War dug in. Langer wears a peace button on his motorcycle helmet.

He is staying here at the pensione pending the arrival of his parents, Dr. and Mrs. Morton Greene of Beverly Hills, who are currently completing a Mediterranean cruise, after which Dr. Greene (chief of Orthopedic Surgery at Cedars of Lebanon Hospital) will spend the remainder of the winter donating his talents in Surgical Procedures to the Florence Medical Institute. They have rented a villa up on via Piana. Langer thinks Florence is "neat," but St. John's Day School is "ridiculous." "Can you imagine," he says, "they haven't even got a chem lab."

Summer and heat release their grip, every degree yielded in a series of savage thunderstorms which clang around the rim of the city's bowl. The last of the summer tourists are departing. The students, the scholars, the hardy *colonisti,* are digging in for the winter occupation. At American Express they smile clubbily over the queued heads at the mail girl, calling *qual' cosa per me?* in mint-fresh accents. They lounge carelessly at the banking table opening their lire checking accounts, converting Daddy's filthy old B of A dollars into Pla-Money. They terminate each transaction with offhand *grazie molto's* ("you're welcome," says the Florentine teller meanly). In piazza Signoria they lounge on the Loggia steps peeling figs, holding their rancid *Nazionales* between thumb and forefinger the way the Italian workmen do. They are elaborately unencumbered. Frisk them and you'll find nothing on them but an AmEx card, a pocketful of lire, and the telephone number of their new girlfriend's pensione, with the 7s carefully crossed.

On the Ponte Vecchio the hippie colony waits with weary, apprehensive eyes, strumming their guitars softly, dozing with their heads propped on knapsacks or on each others' bellies; the point of no honorable return is approaching with the Florentine winter, which they sense will be bitter and inhospitable. They laugh softly among themselves, passing their stubby roaches from hand to hand. The girls' stares are defiant under lank shadows of hair. Their laughter is sudden and wild. The hippie girls dance barefoot on the Ponte Vecchio, insolently wagging their hip-huggered hips at the Florentine gent in his camel greatcoat who strolls by of a late amber afternoon, mistress on one arm and cane on the other, inspecting earrings in the *gioielleria* windows. "What are things coming to?" hisses the mistress, taking a firmer grip on her protector's arm. She shoots the little hippie girl a freezing glare. Oh, it will be cold.

Autumn used to be the time of year I liked best. Gold and scarlet: the first crisp blaze of leaves on the lawn, the first bright leap of flame on the hearth. We walked together, he and I, over the campus to meet our first classes; parted smiling before our respective doors; opened them with a leap of hope upon the first blaze of youthful faces. The old season of youth, of hope, of beginnings.

Here it begins with the sudden hard glare of vitreous frost, into which I set out alone.

3 fall

Behind me, seated at the head of the long table, the lengthening light throws its old cold mantle of authority over my shoulders. Beyond the tall windows the twigs slowly stiffen in the garden. In front of me the ring of expectant faces, waiting to be fed their first ration of hi-protein sani-pakt gov't-inspected regurgitated worm. It is time to begin.

The mood's been established: a loose, cagey sense of group. I'm always a quarter-hour late to a first session. It gives them time to form a little protective clot; balances out the authority figure, permits them to speak out of the security of tribe. Then I arrive slightly flustered, a bit of warmth and charm, calms the nerves, disarms — never mind, I can afford it: authority is a golden thread I long ago learned how to knot. Meanwhile we all see who we're dealing with . . . "How's the scene at Berkeley now," says one young man with a goatee. "I unnerstand the Movement's lost uh impetus, Savio and the rest pretty much outside the uh scene, things at Chicago, I'm at Chicago, things at Chicago are —" "Mrs. Sutherland, I wonder if you know my uncle? He teaches Comparative Lit at Stanford —" "— wanna know if it's OK I just audit? I mean my major's Art," says the pretty little redheaded girl, "but Gary here says I could give him some nonintellectualized feedback —" "Mr. Ferini says you're writing a book," drawls an Ivy League smoothie; "can we expect" — he coughs sharply into his fist — "the woman's point of view on Political History?" "A book, oh wow," snarls a long elegant chick in long inelegant blue jeans, "with the *woman's* point of view. What's the title?"

To the smoothie I say with a smile, "I'm not sure there's such a thing as a woman's point of view, which is what you" — casting the smile at Blue Jeans — "are questioning. It might be rather like saying there's a blond point of view as opposed to the brunette," and continuing to smile at the young man to show that I'm not being didactic nor attempting instruction and that I see him as a *person* even if he's here as a student and that the difference in our experience education and age is to me irrelevant to the discussion at hand etc. — continuing to smile into the smooth gaze paleblue as shallow water I go on to answer the girl's question. "The title of the book, or the working title anyway, is —"

What?

"The title is —"

Click the lock clicks closed. I grope for the Question. How can I provide the Answer when the Question is locked up? I grope around in the shallow water of the paleblue gaze; it freezes, resistantly. I grope from gaze to gaze down the frieze of young faces, waiting for the Answer, waiting to be supplied the Question, and a thin skin of resistance — hey, doesn't she *know?* — ices over each; I grope my way far down to the end of the table at which I arrive at a deep moatblue gaze; no ice and I plunge in, and scrabbling back up for a toehold I hit a large central promontory which is this big kid's nose. I dig my gaze in there and take in a breath of air and continue, "The title is not yet decided. Young man, would you mind shoving that ashtray up here?"

I lounge back, light a cigarette, and propose we discover a Question.

"It has been said that a 'new sensibility has been proclaimed in which the rational, insofar as it is admitted at all, is subordinate to the sensory' . . ."

"I dig that. It's like, you know, nonlinear." Miss Natalie Poirer, all lanky linears and acute angles, picks with long elegant fingers at a patch on the knee of her blue jeans. Angles me an acute look. She is elaborately contemptuous of the rational.

". . . It has been said that the Western mind sees the Universe in terms of edges, while the Eastern sees it in terms of flows. Western society and religion, then, seem to proceed along a line of cause/effect . . ."

The line of disciples, here, a frieze of della Robbia faces, smooth, slippery, carved out of Ivory soap; they are listening now, thawed of the ice skin.

". . . Utopias, depriving us of edges, urgencies, frictions, create at first a panicked society, then a bored one; this is the danger stage as it is still hooked to the rational —"

Care to unhook from the rational, Nose? It is a firm hook, that frowning promontory down at the end of the table, crowning the big red block H on the black sweater. (Not Harvard. So where, my goodness, else . . . ?)

". . . which creates a drag on the evolution to the theoretically higher, or hallucinatory, state —"

"Implying," nips in Goatee, who finally sees his chance to show how things are done at Chicago, "that the hallucinatory society is the optimum one? Theoretically of course."

"Wow," breathe the little girls. There is a general furtive hunching over notebooks (*the drug scene: Utopia?*) and the air in here begins to stretch, strain, creak.

SNORT That would come from all the way down the Nose and around some gnarled cartilage. I tilt my chair, elevate my eyebrows, suggest, "Your spin, Mr. Hatch?"

"I would like to point out," the Nose says in stern and rockbound New England inflections, "that an optimum society is one that deals most effectively with reality."

"Yeah, but what is reality?" Goatee hunches his shoulders and spreads his fingers dialectically. "I mean let's define our terms here. Speaking mechanistically —"

"Shit. Linear shit, that's reality," snaps Miss Poirer. "Reality's a linear hallucination."

"Well, but, like, don't we need the linear?" The Redhead is leaning her bosom earnestly on the table. "I mean like in Art, for instance, isn't linearity what holds, um, everything together?" On the table beside her is her very first sketch of the Baptistery, depicted as a pentagon.

Time to get back to the Question, tighten the golden thread, lasso the errant fragments. "OK," I say. "The point. Let's ask if . . ."

What?

"Let's ask if the idea of . . ."

What? What idea? My God Arabella you've been doing this for years, you can do it in your sleep, you can do it hanging by your knees from the

Nose. Great hunting ax it is, looks as if it's been broken a couple of times, authoritative, Alexander the Great must have had such a nose, he was only a kid himself

"OK, the point. Mr. Hatch has proposed that the optimum society is one that deals most effectively with reality. Next time we'll try to define three terms: optimum, effective, and reality." I dismiss them and it is over.

The big kid gets himself together slowly, methodically. He is the last to leave the table. He rises; it is like the elevation of Mount Rushmore. He ponders. "I wanna say," he pronounces as I gather my notes and my ballpoint pen and my cigarettes and my purse and my coat, "the class is gonna be interesting. I'm a History major but I've never had a course that seemed like it was starting so far back. What I mean, I get the sense of a new beginning. What history may have been before it became History." Frowning speculatively he holds the door open for me. Fatigue fills my bones (all the way from the beginning; my God, me lugging History on my back like a bag of rattly old bones and all these kids waiting for me to pull them out one by one and present them like rattles to play with, to gnaw on, to teethe on) but I smile at him politely as he stands there politely holding open the door.

Thank you, I say.

My pleasure, he says.

"Mangia, mangia." The old Signora, wistful and motherly, urges chicken salad on Langer, who's mounded his plate to haystack height and is well into it. He lifts his head, oil dripping from his underlip. The old Signora smiles sadly. *"Come Mario,"* she murmurs, *"com' un' angelino."* It seems Mario, too, ate like an angel. Mario had a beautiful digestion. *Veramente* he could eat anything —

"Who's Mario?" Mavis wants to know.

"Nyazz," says Ugo abruptly, which is his way of announcing his Dinner Lecture Series. "One day when I was a boy on sum-mer ho-li-day at the farm of my aunt I bicycled ma-ny miles and became very tired. Oh. I was very hun-gry! That evening I ate an en-tire chick-en."

We wait. *"Un pollo intero,"* Ugo repeats, with heavy emphasis. We wait; but it seems this is the entire lecture. *Intero.* We eat.

"Who," says Mavis presently, "is Mario?"

"Com' un' angelo," the Signora moans, touching her pearls and rolling up her amber eyeballs. *"Eeeh Mario, Mario,"* and a tear rolls dryly down her cheek.

"Un pollo intero," roars Ugo, hammering down the lid on another chapter of Brunelli History.

"Have ye not known? Have ye not heard? Hath it not been told to you from the beginning? Isaiah, eleven-twenty-one. Have you-all heard the news about Jesus?"

I look up — up, up — into the sun, if there were a sun on this dreary afternoon. Not the sun but a dazzling sunflower smile, blooming atop a stalk tall as a campanile. The girl must be seven feet tall. She is wearing what seems to be a white chenille bedspread with a hole cut out of the middle. "Uh — not recent news," I mutter.

"Old news, recent news, sweet Jesus is always *good* news," chimes the Campanile, "because He loves you and love's always good news." She bends over me tenderly and presses a pamphlet into my hand, squeezing it, and sings *"By knowledge shall the chambers be filled with all precious and pleasant riches,* Proverbs twenty-four-eleven, so rejoice, you hear?" and she drifts majestically away across the piazza, the way a campanile would do.

Late one rainy evening after staying at the school library to work I'm driving home down via Bolognese and my Fiat lights pick up the Nose, Mr. Peter Hatch, loping down the hill; nobody else is that big or wears, even in the rain, that black sweater with the red block H emblazoned across back and chest. He's hunched up with his hands in his pockets, loping along deep in speculation. I pull over and offer him a lift. Without breaking stride or looking up he mutters *"Non stasera, Signorina."* My face heats. I ram the car into gear and roar off down the hill. By the time I turn into via Cavour I am grinning. What woman my age would mind — in the dark, in the rain — being mistaken for a lady of delights? But by the time I've parked and am fumbling with my key at the palazzo's outer gates my face is hot again. Was there a senile tremor in my voice? Did this arrogant stripling get the impression that the anonymous lady was, so to speak, over the hump?

At exactly 10:20 A.M. a certain light shafts into the right nave of the church of Santa Trinità and strikes to radiant life the Ghirlandaio frescoes of St. Francis. It seems I am not the only goof-off who's discovered this. Waiting alone in the vaulted dimness under the balcony I see a figure come through the curtained door, stump up the empty aisle, halt abruptly at the chapel steps; the shaft strikes, illuminating the frescoed faces — august, transcendent — and the fierce bulldog countenance of Mavis. I regard the girl regarding the Saint; the light seems to gather, strengthening, upon the frescoed visage; and the girl's face gathering its gaze upon it strengthens slowly into a blaze of light; and the Mavian becomes Franciscan, august, transcendent.

The globe turns, the spoke of light wheels past, the blaze ebbs, the dusky silence closes down again. The dumpy figure stands a moment; then with a squaring of the shoulders it turns abruptly and stumps out. I stand listening to the hollow thunk of the footsteps until they have departed, and an old monk shuffles in to begin sweeping the stones with a broom made of twigs.

"Listen. I want to apologize about the other night." I look up from the *Nazione;* Langer and Mavis pause in their bickering over who gets the last rice cake. He looms over the table blocking out half the tearoom with his huge red block-H. "It didn't hit me until you drove off that it was you who'd offered me the lift." Hatch stands with his knee cocked, leaning slightly forward from the hips on which his fists are planted in a referee's stance. The effect is like sitting under an overhanging cliff. He has grown possibly a couple more inches since last Tuesday.

"Sit down," I command. He does so.

"I *say*." Mavis stabs her finger at an extra chair. "Take two. They're small, y'know."

"Jesus," mutters Langer, squinting speculatively. "You play center?"

"Guard. Listen, please accept my apologies for being rude. I didn't recognize you in that car."

"Where," Langer wants to know.

"Nowhere this year. I busted my knee. You play?"

"Not this year," says Langer laconically. "Just prep school, anyway."

"I s'pose we ought to get a fresh pot of tea," says Mavis to the air. "No telling who might want some."

I make introductions. Hatch and Greene exchange a manful shake. "What position?" Hatch asks Greene. "Quarterback," Greene says. "Quarterback, pretty classy," says Hatch in congratulatory tones. "Yeah, well, just prep school," scowls Langer, looking smug. "Would anybody care for some rice cakes?" Mavis says somewhat loudly. Hatch contemplates; then shakes his head. Mavis says "My treat, of course," scowling airily upward; and Hatch says "Well yeah then, thanks, Mavis," and settles in for some serious discussion with Langer on the necessity for football players of keeping the legs in shape. The thing to do, they agree, is to run in sand.

Here Rest
The Remains of

MARIO NICCOLÒ BRUNELLI
1925   1944

Struck Down in the
Flower of His Youth
for

GOD,   COUNTRY,   HUMANITY

He Waits for Us
IN PARADISE

"Good grief. Where'd you find it, Mavis?"

"The graveyard up behind San Miniato. Stumbled over it quite literally, couldn't b'lieve my eyes. This marble statue, life-size, nekkid chap lying flat out on his tum, fallen with this torch in his hand. Most lifelike thing, spotted this bare bum sticking up amongst the weeds. White as snow. Frightfully embarrassing, really. Must've cost them simply *pounds,* life-size marble, carved with absolutely every wrinkle on the soles of the feet, life-size." She looks genuinely shaken. "Shouldn't be surprised if that's what happened to the last of their fortune. Frightful, really, what these Catholics put into their filthy religion. Wouldn't be so appalling if it were a decent piece of *Art.*"

Fiat has done more for the Italian than merely improve his economy. It has placed in his hands another means of expressing his *machismo*. Last night I had a right-of-way showdown with some old gramps and wound up with my new car crumpled against a pillar. I climbed out, shaking with fury. The sirens started to wail. A crowd began to gather. If I'd stayed I might have wound gramps around the pillar. I opted for the better part of valor and walked away into the dark.

So this afternoon there appear at the Brunelli door two of the *polizia's* finest. (Florentine joke: Why do the police always go in pairs? Answer: One to read, the other to write.)

Che trambusto. Ugo, lunching, turns purple and marches to his room; Lina flees to the pantry, where Agata rattles pans fiercely about, issuing warnings that she, at least, will defend the *casa;* the old Signori take to their beds after telephoning the doctor, who rushes over to administer prophylactic injections of penicillin and vitamins; Domi the poodle dashes yipping up and down the corridors.

I closet myself with the *polizia* and a bottle of brandy and after an hour they depart, bowing themselves out with many ceremonious apologies for having invaded the Signora's privacy. It seems that they gained the impression somewhere that the Signora is a friend, a very close friend, of the Barone who owns this palazzo and who is brother-in-law to the mayor.

"You lied to the police?" says Peter Hatch in accents grown severely Bostonian.

"*Madonna,*" mutters Carlo.

"It's cool," Natalie sniffs. "Pigs."

We are in the faculty coffee room, where Carlo and I

confer after our classes and where some of the kids tend to infiltrate — tonight we have Hatch, Natalie, Gary the Goatee, redheaded Sandra.

"What did they say?" Carlo demands irritably. "Did you sign anything?" Carlo is trying to ignore the kids while maintaining both status (what makes these little shits think they can consort with *professori?*) and radical style (in the Movement we spit on artificial elitist class barriers). "Did they write down your statement?"

"I told you, Carlo, the matter's dropped. They just apologized and left."

"Pigs. It's cool," says Natalie.

"*Madonna,* you are such innocents, you foreigners! You are so trusting. Do you actually believe —"

"Stupid. The pigs are the same everywhere — stupid." Natalie contemptuously stirs her coffee with a long forefinger.

"— they will let this matter drop? That they will not attempt to persecute you?"

"You mean prosecute." Hatch's frown is mildly incredulous. "You mean your police'd prosecute a woman for walking away from a car accident? I mean, she shouldn't have lied, but —"

"Lied. That's cool."

"It may be cool but it's not very sensible," says Hatch, turning his sensible frown from me to her.

"Oh wow, sensible," she says with an acid drip of laugh, "you sensible men, always so damn respectful of petty authority."

"Yeah, well, you women don't get thrown in jail too often.

You might consider that," Hatch points out in a fatherly way. "Women get by with a lot more sass."

"I am warning you," chatters Carlo, "this *radicalità femminile,* in Italy you do not get by with this shit."

"Oh?" Natalie is eying Carlo dangerously. "Gee, Mr. Ferini, I was under the impression you were, like, really into the *radicalità* thing. I mean I didn't figure you to be so uptight about a little hassle with the pigs. Or maybe it's just women you Italians don't take shit from?"

"He's only pointing out," says Hatch, pointing his big beak all unknowing into the line of crossfire, "that theory's one thing, practicality's another. It doesn't matter if cops are stupid or not or if you're a woman or not, you lie to them, you can get busted."

Natalie is slowly stroking the patch on her jeans with a long sharp fingernail. "Tell me. Have *you* ever been busted?"

"Nope," says Hatch mildly.

"Yeah, it was a stupid question, wasn't it?" She grins. Her teeth look long, sharp. "They'd never bust an Establishment type like you, would they? With his football sweater and his neat haircut and his really cool Kennedy accent. *He'd* never lie to the cops. It wouldn't be *practical.* I mean" — she takes a deep breath to steady her fury, for she's into it now and she can't stop and she has to make it work for her — "they can beat up demonstrators and use tear gas and nightsticks on us impractical radicals who'd sort of like to see us stop using bombs and napalm on the Gooks, I mean we'd all really like to make them stop doing that, only we should work through the System, shouldn't we, and cooperate with the cops and quit lying and do it with rational *discourse* instead of getting our heads busted? I mean let's stay *rational* and work it through the good old System and preserve the holy Constitution and the sanctity of our institutions, home and family and womanhood, keep ourselves clean and straight-arrow so we can win this one for the Gipper. Yeah, clean mind in a clean body, no smoking or drinking or using hash or fucking just for the fun of it, that wouldn't be *practical,* gotta stay in *condition* so we can lead the team to glory and maybe they'll let you volunteer for the Green Berets —"

Standing looking from her face to Hatch's, which is slowly covering with a glaze, like porcelain in the kiln's heat, I suddenly recognize that what this girl is howling is not politics but sex; she has heard the click of some lock and this kid, this Hatch, has inadvertently turned it and absentmindedly and innocently pocketed the key. *Somebody is going to suffer for this,* she rages; *he is going to suffer for this.*

I move instinctively, protectively, toward her, touch her shoulder. She twists away. "You too," she snarls. "You think you keep the goddam *discourse* open, you think you're objective but what you're teaching is the old Establishment gas, the old linear *rationality* — Oh fuck it," and she stalks out.

"You see what happens," stutters Carlo into the silence, "when women try to discuss politics?"

Means of goofing off work are not limitless. Museums are closed on Monday and the dimness of unlit churches has begun to remind me of my dimming years; in a few weeks I shall be forty. And what then? A brooding staleness comes to settle in my mind, locked up tight behind the old block, while each day I rummage doggedly through my notes for the key. I awake some nights with my unused youth roosting on my brow like a bald black condor. It smells of low tide.

Fresh air, I command myself; *walk.* I trudge up the Viale, dead leaves rustling like tissue under my boots; a chill wind swirls up off the Arno.

Piazzale Michelangelo: the statue of David, green as a frog, stares coldly, coyly, over his shoulder out past the cypressed slope of the Belvedere, the rim of hills beyond which lies old enemy Pisa. The city is no young giant-killer anymore; it has aged, turned dun, respectable, monumental; a monumental bag of old stones and bones. (And I? If not monumental then respectable, dun.) I light a cigarette and stand at the wall gazing out over the needled turrets, domes, crenellations, the old goldmaned Duomo crouched like a lion in its heraldic litter of bones.

"Scusi. Ha fiammifero?" I turn. The young buck is grinning; it is not that kind of match he wants. Fixing him with a dun, respectable glare I hand him a packet of *cerini* and stalk off.

Huh. Huh. *Huh.* HUH. Halfway down the Viale and coming up fast behind me: the young buck? Running? Nonsense. I turn up my collar, quicken my stride. *Huh.* HUH. HUH. *Huh.* And he has sped on by, the sough of his breath and his footfall fading as he streaks down through the trees, scarlet block H blurring like a taillight as he disappears.

"Pisa: massimo, *tzee*-ro; minima, *mee*-nus ot-to. Milano: massimo, *mee*-nus quatro, minima —" From Ugo's weather report, quoted directly from the *Nazione,* we are to gather that it is too cold, much too cold for a picnic. And even if not cold — which, repeat, it will be — a picnic is quite impossible. Is it not November? Have not the furnaces been fired? What manner of pagan *festa* is this Thanksgiving, that it must be celebrated in so dangerous a manner?

"The beach. Wonkiest thing I ever heard of," snorts Mavis.

"Sand," mumbles Langer. "Best place to get the legs in shape."

"*Sand?*" roars Mavis. "*Legs?*"

"You see any sand around town?" says Langer reasonably.

"Come along if you'd like, Mavis," I say. "I'm giving the new car a spin. A few of the students are coming, and bringing stuff for a picnic, and then we're going to Pisa."

"Well, the Cathedral's worth seeing," says Mavis grudgingly. She's been dying to be invited. "Pisano's tabernacle of course."

"Americans," Ugo announces, "eat duck on this *festa*. Oh. Once when I was a boy at the farm of my aunt —"

"Not duck. Goose," declares Mavis.

"Nononono," Ugo quacks. "Duck."

"Oh no. Goose, definitely, *goose,*" thunders Mavis.

We shall overcooooome,
We shall overcooooome,
We shall overcome
Some daaaaaaay.

snapping like a banner behind us as we tear down the autostrada. Sprung from stony old Florence for the first time — has it been almost three months? — into the sudden openness of road and flat low fields, everybody reverts. Langer lips a harmonica; Gary the Goatee abandons cool, dandles delicious Sandra on his lap, belts out teenybopper tunes; Mavis's pugilistic scowl takes on a benign nursemaidy aspect; even Pete mumbles along in an uneven but pure baritone. And I — I find I've opened up the new Peugeot to an exuberant 130 kph. It holds the road nicely, my new anti-*machismo* machine; it should, loaded with this weight.

We will not be swaaaaayed,
We will not be swaaaaayed,

as we sway wildly down the autostrada.

Cold: the beach at Viareggio is as predicted. Long barren strand straggling out of thin pines. Abandoned promenade (SWIM! PLAY! DANCE!) giving way to huddles of empty dressing huts. But off come the kids' shoes and socks, yelling they hobble over pebbles and broken glass down to the cold sand, break in sprints for the water — *cold, cold!* — but it is the sea, it is the old Mediterranean.

Escorted by gentlemanly Mr. Hatch, Mavis and I pick

our way sedately, filling shoes with cold sand. I sit on a log to remove them. Mavis plops, puffing, beside me. "Silly asses. Wading in the sea in November."

"Go on," I say to Pete, "go run your ten miles."

He takes off like a spring. Mavis and I sit on the log and watch him recede, knees pumping high, elbows tucked economically in against his ribs.

"Chap's a bit wiggy, if you ask me," sniffs Mavis. "Shouldn't be s'prised if he twisted an ankle."

Down at the shore Langer and Gary and Sandra are whooping, splashing water. Mavis nudges me. "Look at that. He *is* going to twist an ankle." Pete has veered, swiveled, ramming out an arm at an imaginary tackler, sprinting back again toward us.

"Football," Mavis snorts. "Men. Honestly."

Football. I look away, embarrassed for something I can't name. For a simpler, quixotic, departed world (*Football, my students would say; God, those jocks*)? For my father, who is dead? My brother, who is not?

(*Snapshot, taken in the late thirties:* Arabella's brother Buddy in knickers and an airplane helmet standing on the running board of their father's new Packard. It is Buddy's birthday and he is holding a football the father has given him. It is a genuine regulation football. He smiles sincerely into the camera . . . He thanked my father properly, I remember — Gee whiz a football, Oh boy that's keen Dad, thank *you* — and had his picture taken with it and then put it on his bureau, where it stayed until he got married. If my father, who equated manliness with team sports and team sports with what he called "intestinal fortitude," felt

any disappointment with my brother, he kept it to himself.
My father must have come to understand, eventually, that
the authority of manhood was no longer considered to re-
side in fists nor intestines; but sometimes I saw him looking
down at his hands, and as he flexed them, opening and
closing his fists, a look of bewilderment would come over
him . . .)

"I say, shall I fetch the picnic? It *is* getting on t'ward
noon, you know. They'll probably be famished when they
get back."

I wander barefoot down to the water. The Mediterranean
here is gray. Wavelets wash in feebly; the shells are made of
overused elements, stunted and thin as babies' fingernails.
I remember California beaches, resonant with surf, booming
with power; I remember great gross conches, enormous fans
of coral, giant squid, forests of kelp like redwoods. I remember being young, running on the beach.

I find myself running. My startled lungs gasp, falter,
gasp again — and I am running.

"Where? Knee? Ankle? Where's it hurt? Show me."

On one knee beside me, panting, dripping sweat, he bends
over me. "Where?" he demands.

Where did he come from and who asked *him?* I grab my
leg back out of his paws. "It's all *right*," I pant furiously.

"It's not all right. You fell funny. Looks to me as if the
ankle —"

"Funny as it looked, Mr. Hatch, I'm OK. And I can get
up by myself. I haven't broken a *hip* or anything."

"Hip? Did you hurt your hip?"

That's what us old ladies tend to do, sonny, break our brittle old hips. *"No,"* I snarl. So he hauls me up, sets me on my feet, holds me steady, looks me over. "Can you stand?" "Anything but being fussed over. Please. You're acting as if I'd tumbled out of my wheelchair."

I turn and stalk off. Ankle grinds glass shards but I do not limp. It is ridiculous. It is humiliating. It is OOF. He grabs my arm and hauls me back up. "Listen," he says irately, "you can ruin yourself, trying to walk on a bad ankle."

I heave a strangled sigh. "But coach," I whine, "I wanna stay in the game."

He grins. "The guy who bombs and runs away —"

"Lives to play another day. OK, coach. Your arm, then. I guess I've lost this game."

"A great man once said, 'You don't lose games, you just —' "

" 'run out of time.' I know."

"Hey, you do know. Where did you —"

"Listen sonny," I say rapidly because my teeth have begun clacking, "you don't have to play football to know that. You just have to start running out of time."

"Let me say this," he says as we limp off down the beach, "you may not have the weight but you got the guts."

I do? I feel a flush of gratitude. "Why, thank you."

"My pleasure."

We shall overcooooome,
We shall overcooooome,

Overcome with fatigue, food, fresh air, I watch the auto-strada flow into the gray dusk. The kids sing softly, slumped in a tangle, like puppies. Pete drives with the benign savagery of young men who do not understand machinery and are quite convinced they've mastered it.

Warmed, aerated, the pain at a comfortable distance, I close my eyes, let my head rest on the back of the seat. Let myself be borne back home on the sweet sleepy young voices.

"Did I not tell you," Ugo says, "it would be danger-ous?"

Walk, says Dr. Mori, who despite his name seems to have a vital interest in my ankle (No, Dr. Mori; you have lovely teeth, you turn a lovely compliment, and I understand why all the nice young Fulbright wives suffer these epidemics of palpitations; but I understand also that you have a wife, Dr. Mori; and despite the length of my hem and my black stockings I am quite the Victorian about such things). So I walk, and I walk alone.

A glum day only an American would walk abroad in. Up on deserted piazzale Michelangelo — I am a creature of habit these days, I make the same *giro* — standing by the wall, looking out over the City: a familiar back. I tap the shoulder. *"Scusi. Ha fiammiferi, Signore?"*

He turns, refusal already politely formed in the stern & rockbound aspect, *non stasera, Signorina.* "Hey." He registers. Then frowns. "Listen, you go around doing that, you'll get yourself in trouble. What if I'd turned out to be a strange Italian?" I stifle a grin (what if he'd turned out to be a

strange elephant?) and say, "What kind of trouble?"
"Never mind," he says darkly, "just don't do it."

"I really do need a match."

"Smoking ruins the wind." Scowling, he lopes off into
the mist. Whippersnapper. Presumes to pass judgment on
my wind. I shrug; turn to look out over the City.

A tap on my shoulder; he hands me a pack of *cerinis*.

"Why, thank you, Pete. Where'd you snitch them?"

"I didn't snitch them. I bought them over at that bar."

"Well, thanks. How much? Let me —"

"Twenty lire."

I give him twenty lire: 3.2 cents. "Thank you," he says,
pocketing it.

"My, uh, pleasure." It is indeed, to see the verification of
what one had thought myth: oldfashioned New England
thrift. "How's the ankle?" he says. "Fine. How's the knee?"
"As good as it'll ever be," he says, "but I'll never play football again." He says it matter-of-factly, but with an overtone
of sorrow. I consider saying that that is what it comes to,
eventually: as we grow older we find that there are more
and more things we shall never do again. But I don't. Who
needs to be instructed in sorrow?

A fine sweet rain has begun to fall. We stand surveying
the city. The chivalric crenellations, the great lion couchant.
"Some town," he says. "It is that," I say.

Presently he heaves a sigh. "Right now I'm supposed to
be at the Uffizi, with that so-called Art History class. It's a
drag. The instructor, that Englishwoman —" He reddens.
"Sorry. I guess she's a friend of yours."

"Colleague, is all. I hear she's a bore."

He shoots me a grateful glance. "Let's put it this way. She about had me turned off on the entire Renaissance. Everything so radiant this and beautiful that. Pretty soon those Madonnas begin to look like a bunch of women fresh out of a beauty parlor. And those della Robbias, she can make you see your mother's Wedgwood ashtrays. You get what I'm saying?"

"Yes." A vivid picture of my mother's Wedgwood ashtrays.

"I figure you've gotta make your own response, right?"

"Right."

"So I started looking into it on my own. I like to do my own evaluating. If I'm told something's famous it might bias me," says this heir to Transcendentalism, relodging the proposition that a true knowledge of all things material and immaterial is at least possible.

He squints out, evaluating, over old stony Florence. "Some of this stuff, it's . . ." he plunges deep into his pockets for the word ". . . moving." And having found it swallows it like a large whole oyster. "Although some of it, for instance a lot of that stuff in the Pitti, hits me as a waste of time. Digging all of it out for yourself, there's a lot of hit and miss, a lot of waste. I hate waste," he says, bleakly. "There's not enough time to waste on things."

The rain has strengthened. I drop my cigarette, turn up my coat collar. "Did you ever happen onto those jars of bones," I say, "in the little rooms behind the Medici Chapel altar?"

4 *winter*

Child's Guide to Culture:

We dive into the shelter of the tearoom, shuck our dripping coats.

Langer: What were you, swimming in the Arno?

Goatee: Hatch, will you pick just one person to drip on?

Mavis: Ew, you're getting the cakes all soggy.

Arabella: Oof. My ribs ache. I haven't had laughs like that in years.

Pete: More like bellows. I never knew such a small woman could make so much noise. She almost got us booted out of the Pitti for disturbing the sacramental peace.

Sandra: Laughing? At Art? Oh wow.

Mavis (contemptuously): The Pitti. Oh.

Langer (knowingly): Oh, the Pitti. You saw that baboon, I bet.

Mavis: Full of junk, the Pitti. The ceilings. Those cabinets. The ivories. Hideous.

Gary: What baboon?

Langer: The one painted on the ceiling. You look right up into its

Pete: Never mind.

Langer: ass, and its balls are painted

Pete: I said *never mind.*

Langer: blue. Christ, Hatch, you think Art should be rated like movies? X for kids under 18?

Pete: No. There's ladies present, is all. (stunned silence)

"Nyazz. From the left of the third gal-ler-y there opens out the fa-mous cor-ridor constructed by Vasari in 1564, on a com-mis-sion from Cosimo I, which links the —"

Ugo's evening lecture is occasioned by my mention of the Guided Culture Tour I am giving, and have just offered by extension to Mavis. To my surprise she turns me down.

"Seems to me you're making a joke of it," she scowls. "Can't think how you imagine it's instructive. Going 'round pointing out wonky things like reliquaries stuffed with bones and frightful ceilings and wretched fourth-rate paintings like the *Ecce Homo* and that Sebastiano full of arrows like a porcupine, nobody can take any of it *seriously* —"

"That's the point, Mavis. If you start out by taking everything seriously, you wind up —"

"Room XXI. Nyazz. The *Sacred Allegory* by Giovanni —"

"— like that," I murmur.

"Tell us, Ugo," Mavis snaps, "when were you last in the Uffizi?"

Poor Ugo. Unable to abandon scholarship to learn the lesson. "There are too ma-ny tou-rists," he quacks.

Of whom Mavis, it seems, is *numera una*. She manages with efficient regularity to bully her way into the most cloistered, jealously guarded *sancta* very few Italians and almost no tourists ever enter. She has inspected the fore-mentioned corridor — closed to the public for years — that runs from the Uffizi over the old bridge to the Pitti; in it are stored, she says, "a few rather int'resting pieces." She is beginning to find the hassle inconvenient. She has lodged a complaint with the "authorities" decrying the matter of Italian Art in general and in specific noting the closing of certain rooms in the Uffizi, making unavailable for inspection those treasures which have been placed in storage because of lack of funds for their proper display. "Lack of business methods, *I* say," snaps Mavis. "If they can't afford to show the pieces why don't they simply sell off a few so they can mount the rest properly?"

"Sell them?" roars Ugo; "part with the Art which is our Na-tio-nal Trea-sure?"

"Fat lot of good it does you locked away in the basement," says Mavis sensibly.

Langer's parents have arrived. They're now in residence in the villa up on via Piana, where Langer has an entire floor with his older brother Seth. Invited up for cocktails — at, thank God, the sensible American hour of six, and with canapés instead of bonbons — I find that bright brash eminently comfortable kind of Jewish bourgeoisie I feel easiest with. Eleanor Greene is Executive Director of a privately endowed Mental Health Foundation in Los Angeles — a small plump bouncy little dynamo of a woman who chews gum exuberantly ("I quit *SNAP* smoking a year ago, it's still *POP* hell. I dint realize how *oral* *POP SNAP* I was") and wears neon-green eyeshadow and false eyelashes like beach umbrellas and a superstructure of gold wire which she says is a wig. "Israel was a gas," she says, "all the kibbutz gals flipped over the eyelashes, I ordered a couple dozen pairs sent over from Bullock's for them."

Dr. Morton Greene has a round tan face and kindly tan eyes and wears a maroon blazer and black silk turtleneck into which his jowls are neatly tucked. He mixes a neat very dry American martini and passes glasses around on a tray. Then he passes around a bowl of cashews; then the platter of canapés; then he goes to a console and puts on a selection of records, adjusting all the sound knobs; then he goes around again with the martini pitcher offering refills. Then he passes around the bowl of cashews, the platter of canapés . . .

A tallish scrawny woman sweeps in followed by Langer's brother Seth, who's been giving her a tour of the villa. "I'll be damned if you haven't got four decent *bath*rooms," she cries, "gawd Ellie if that isn't just *like* you, grabbing the only villa in Florence with four *decent* johns," and to me, "*I* spend half my life trying to track down the basic necessities here and *she* dashes off a note from California and nabs the only villa in — thanks Morty-baby — Florence that's *live*able. My gawd. Lox. And bagels. Wouldn't you *know*.

Here two days and she finds lox. Ellie you drive me up the *wall*. You know what we had for Thanksgiving? Pheasant. Could I find a turkey? One single little *tacchino*? Combing every little *polleria* practically as far as Arezzo? She de*feats* me." She throws herself sprawling onto the couch. "Four johns for gawd's sake."

"The supermarket down around . . ." Eleanor waves her hand vaguely ". . . you know, the outskirts, it's got *POP* practically everything, like an American *SNAP* Safeway."

"Oh well if you want to come to Italy and do your shopping in a *super*market," and the scrawny woman jangles her bangles contemptuously.

Maggi Miller (I gather) is a Beverly Hills expatriate divorcée and artist who got fed up to *here* with America and Ronnie Reagan and LBJ barbeques and redneck mentality and of course the War and the persecution of the blacks; it got so that she had to take two tranquilizers every morning before she could bring herself to open the L.A. *Times.* "Even the people I *knew, my friends,* all they were doing was just standing around at parties *talk*ing. Nobody ever *did* anything — except you of course, Ellie sweetie, you worked your little *ass* off for that crisis center —" So she split. Came to Italy to live. "Oh I know the political system here is simply Mickey Mouse, but I mean how can anybody in *con*science continue to live in the United States, the way things *are?*" She takes a sip of her martini. Closes her eyes, leans her head back against the couch. "Oh gawd it is so *good* to have somebody hand you a *proper* martini again," she groans.

Langer's brother Seth is a thinnish stooped young man of about twenty with a thinnish beard and thinnish shoulder-length hair, wearing faded blue jeans and work shirt and a very heavy bronze peace medallion on a very heavy chain, which may account for the stoop. He has a gentle, somewhat blurred smile. He slopes over to me and opens a flat gold cigarette case in which are clamped four handrolled tubes. "You, uh, smoke?" he says in a soft voice. I smile, shake my head. "Very good Moroccan stuff," he says. I say it'd be wasted on me, all I get is a sore lip. "I guess I'm pretty much a member of the booze generation," I add, trying to make it regretful but not apologetic. He shrugs and smiles. "Yeah," he murmurs, "I guess when you're into one thing, that's the thing you're into," and slopes out to the kitchen to see if there's any ice cream left.

"Americans overtip," Maggi Miller is saying to Morton. "Don't think they don't *laugh* at you for it. Remember, they've already added fifteen percent service charge to the tab, even in the cheap *trattorie*. Don't let them *con* you."

Child's Guide to Culture, cont'd: The Uffizi

In the room with the six panels of the Virtues, Peter Hatch stands in front of the easel which holds back-to-back the two little Botticelli paintings, one of the slain Holofernes and the other of Judith bearing off his head. Eying the decapitated torso he mutters, "Man. Look at the build on that guy. I mean he is really in *shape*."

Later, stalking redfaced down the Galleria corridor: "That guard — did he think noise was going to damage the paintings? Jesus. I'd like to know what broke you up. I mean what's so hilarious about Botticelli?"

Ugo is out on strike. He disapproves of *sciopero* — when Mussolini was in power no such disruptions were permitted and all was orderly — but Ugo cannot make a spectacle of himself by being the only one to appear at the office. Nor can he be seen abroad during working hours, for then everybody will assume he is supporting the strike. So he holes up in his room until two o'clock, when it is safe to return to his afternoon routine.

"Still out on strike today, Ugo?" says Mavis at dinner. He pretends not to hear. She repeats the question. A "nyazz" is finally forced out. Mavis smiles, basely triumphant. She's kidding herself if she thinks she's driven home a point. If Ugo were unable to accommodate such obvious dichotomies he would not be a Florentine, not be an Italian, certainly not be Ugo. Above all, one accommodates.

Child's Guide cont'd: San Marco

Pete: A mummified bishop?
Arabella: Under glass.
Pete: His skin looks like a wrinkled brown paper bag. Jesus, the weight of that miter's squashed out his eyeballs.
A: Do you want to guess what became of them?

Pete (pondering): They've got 'em pickled in a jar someplace, right?

A: Right. These are thrifty folk, like New Englanders.

Pete: Yuk yuk. Where are they? The eyeballs.

A: That's for you to discover. Teacher's not supposed to do
all the research.

Pete: "Teacher"? With mummified bishops and pickled
eyeballs you're supposed to be teaching some kind of
course?

A: No. I'm sorry.

Pete: Hey, I didn't offend you, did I?

A: Of course not. I guess I'm apt to think of everything in
terms of teaching.

Pete: I guess I should think of myself in terms of a student,
then. I mean I'm pretty young. Maybe I don't come
through very strong as a person.

A: I wouldn't say that's one of your problems. I'm not
pulling rank on you, Pete. Some of my best friends are
young people.

Pete: Glad to hear you're not a segregationist.

A: And I confess I don't know where those eyeballs are.

Pete: Typical teacher's ploy. "That's for you to discover."
Let the student do the research, huh?

A: The theory is to lead the pupil to the edge of knowledge
and abandon him there.

Pete: Abandon. Listen, no offense, but do we have to go
back to theories of instruction? I'm twenty years old and
I've spent three-quarters of my life being instructed. I
don't think you have to give yourself an excuse just to be
in the company of a

A: I just remembered: I know where there's a pickled fore-
finger.
Pete: A finger? Whose? Some pope's, I suppose.
A: Better: Galileo's. The *middle* finger.
Pete (after pondering): Jesus. Galileo's middle finger. He
really gave it to 'em, didn't he? Beautiful. Now that is
. . . moving. Galileo's middle finger, pointing to the sun.
Yuk-yuk.

Coming out into the courtyard of the Uffizi, we are suddenly engulfed by a *dimonstrazione*. Loudspeakers blaring
martial music, placards demanding POPOLO, LIBERTÀ — the
ancient rallying cry of the Florentine masses (to which the
answer was once a lusty *palle, palle* to signify devotion to
the six red balls of the Medici, I inform Pete. "Yuk-yuk,"
he mutters, unamused). A hard line of wariness along his
jaw, he grabs my elbow and starts to maneuver me around
the edges. I balk: "Wait; let's see what's happening." "You
can see what's happening at a safer distance," he says. And
at that moment the throng surges, closes around us; the
faces — dun, conservative, unvaried in their aspect as a uni-
form, the very familiar and alien face of Florence itself —
become suddenly historic and frightening. With a click not
of intellect but of gut the inscrutable Question is at last
unlocked and I rewitness the dismemberment of old Pazzi's
half-decayed corpse and the stench of Savonarola's roasting
flesh and if I were to look up past these dun faces I would
glimpse the archbishop Salviati hanging from that Palazzo
Vecchio window with his ornate vestments fluttering as he
slowly twirls at the end of his rope. I feel myself jerked up

by the armpits, hoisted aloft and borne levitating and dignified safely back through history's savage faces to the Arno
wall where I am set down, abruptly, on my bottom.

"Oof. Really, Pete, I don't think heroics were called for,
these demonstrations are quite" — redfaced I busily brush
off my coat; did he detect my flash of cowardice? — "common, you know, there's always some —"

"They may be common but a mob's a mob in Italy same
as it is in the U.S. You don't want to mess with any mob."

"Bus-drivers, for heaven's sake, striking for higher retire-
ment pensions — would you mind getting me off this wall
— quite *reasonable* when you consider how underpaid —"

"Sure it's reasonable, most real revolutionary action's reasonable, but that's got nothing to do with how safe it is to
mess around with it."

"*You* think most revolutionary action is reasonable?"
We've started toward the Ponte Vecchio but now I stop. "I
didn't have you down as a radical."

"Yeah, it's how I look." He adds tightly, "With all respect,
I'm getting tired of having people assume my entire charac-
ter from how I look."

"Pete, I didn't mean that. What I assume is from your,
uh, strong sense of practicality. I mean I just can't see you
burning draft-board files."

"I probably would, if it did any good," he says grimly.
"You're right about practicality. That doesn't mean I don't
want things changed — radically. Jesus, I thought you'd
understand that." He jams his hands into his pockets and
trudges on.

I hurry on after him, touch his elbow. "Pete — forgive me.
I wasn't really making that kind of judgment. As a —"

"— teacher, you're objective. I know," he says wearily. "It's OK."

"Hi there. Have y'all said hello to Jesus today?"

I look up — up, up — and there it is, the Campanile with the sunflower smile. "There's still time," she chimes, "to greet sweet Jesus today. Hi there, Pete."

"Hi, Billie Jean. How's business?"

"Oh just fine, fine and dandy. What's all that yellin and carryin-on over at the piazza?"

"Bus-drivers' demonstration. Excuse me — this is Billie Jean, uh —"

"Woodcock. Billie Jean Woodcock. Pleased to meet you. And this here's Sascha."

Where? Emerging from the folds of the bedspread, a very small boy with a raw Russian old-man's face. *"Dì ciao, Sascha,"* smiles the Campanile, *"e dà loro l'opuscolo."* Sascha whispers *ciao* and hands us each a pamphlet and retires behind the bedspread. "Sascha's helpin us, me and Jesus. We're a team for Jesus."

"Bravo Sascha." At the bracing coach's tone the wizened old-man's face reemerges, gazes up, up. Pete bends down, down, gives the hand a manly shake.

"Remember Jesus loves you, so don't y'all be shy about saying hello to Him, you hear? We gotta hustle on over to the demonstration now, so we'll see y'all later."

"Hey wait," says Pete, "listen, Billie Jean, I wouldn't get mixed up in that mob."

"Oh we'll be fine, just fine, all those people in one spot, we can get a whole bunch done, can't we, Sascha?"

"Listen. You wanna use some sense, Billie Jean. You remember what happened last week at that UPIM sale. You

know you, uh, attract attention." Indeed: a few of the
Italians have collected, standing in a ring staring up at this
tableau of titans. "And with that mob — you oughtta be
practical."

"Why now it's sure practical. *When two or three are
gathered together in His name —*"

"Yeah, well, that bunch isn't gathered together in that
name exactly."

"*— there shall He be,*" and she bends upon him a smile
so powerful it would have knocked a smaller man off the
bridge, and appears to vaporize.

"Oh Christ I oughtta go with her," Pete groans.

"He *is* with her. You should know there's nothing anybody can do for someone who's determined to testify. Some
people just buck for it . . . You seem to know her. What
was it you were saying happened last week at UPIM?"

"I shoulda gone with her. She just faded — she does that,
I never saw a girl who could move so fast." He turns; we
amble on across the bridge. "Man, is she light on her feet.
She'd make a fantastic basketball player."

Plied with *paste* and *cioccolata* at the tearoom he finally
allows me to pry out the details of the UPIM caper. It seems
that Billie Jean got herself into a hassle in the department
store, passing out pamphlets to the mobs of shoppers; some
of the women turned ugly, called her a foreigner and a
witch, started clawing at her and shoving her around, at
which Sascha attacked, getting in a few good leg bites, and
then some men started gathering, grinning and jeering,
getting pretty damn fresh, starting to handle her. Seems

Pete, who was shopping for socks (they were on sale but they didn't have his size, he says grumpily), waded in and pried her loose and got her out the employees' door.

— Sometimes I think women don't have any sense. These guys — these *ragazzi* — I mean you get a group of guys horsing around, things sometimes happen. I've seen it.
— Come on, Italian men never really follow through. It's just the *machismo* ritual.
— Italians don't have the franchise. I tell you I've seen these things happen.
— Where? Not in Italy, I bet.
— In New York. Excuse me. I think I'll get a couple more of these . . . (returning) Jesus, they're forty-five lire. Isn't that about ten cents? They're kinda small for
— Seven and a half cents. What were you doing in New York?
— I worked there for a couple of summers. Lord, I thought food was supposed to be cheap in Italy.
— Depends on how much of it you eat. What work were you doing in New York?
— Mostly trying to avoid getting my skull busted. I had, let's see, fifty lire for the chocolate, and 5 times 45 for the
— *Skull* busted? For heaven's sake, Pete, what were you *doing?*
— Working in Harlem. How much is 275 lire in dollars?
— About forty-five cents. Working in the ghetto, you mean? What work?
— Teaching. A Quaker program for junior-high-age kids. Hand me your ticket. I'll take care of it.

— Teaching, why that's splendid, Pete. What did you teach?

— Just about anything. Remedial reading mostly. And athletics. We got a fantastic basketball team together, and baseball, you shoulda seen those little kids, some of them real naturals. That age, you know, they really dig it. Before all these pressures close in on 'em. The thing is to try to keep 'em together, give 'em a sense of *team* . . . Let's see, that's 150 plus 275 lire —

— Give it back, Pete. I'll take care of it.

— Really? Well, thank you.

— My pleasure.

Dr. Greene drives a huge silver Mercedes. "The Mercedes is the finest car made, with the exception of the Rolls," he says. "Doubtless," says Carlo Ferini with a glacial smile. The Greenes and Ferinis and I are winding up a little supper party I've thrown at Camillo's which seemed like a good idea — mixed Jewish liberal and Florentine radical — but has turned out as difficult and convoluted as a Medici convention. "I always wanted a Mercedes but, you know" — the doctor waves his hand — "German-made. Know what I mean?" "Indeed," mutters Carlo with heavy significance. "So then one day I was in surgery at Cedars and I happened to look up at the field light — you know, that floods the surgery. Around the rim there's the name of this German optical firm. I went out that afternoon and ordered the Mercedes for delivery in Milan. Beautifully made car. They last practically forever, you know."

There is a silence. "I understand," Carlo says at last, tightly, "that American automobile companies are secretly controlled by the munitions cartel, so that the plants can be converted momentarily into weapons manufacture."

And *I* understand, if the Greenes do not, that this is as close as Carlo will ever bring himself to offering an out from a glaring ideological gaffe.

Here I sit at the tearoom table presiding over my kindergarten salon. Mavis, Langer, Gary/Sandra, Pete form the nucleus. Occasionally Sascha materializes, seemingly shaken out of Pete's pant-leg to which he has attached himself silently, adoringly, like a little pet Russian bear cub; and once in a while there is one enormous German hippie name of Claus (the Claw) whom Langer has picked up and is training, like an elephant, to play soccer.

It seems Pete and Langer have scraped together a soccer team: themselves and the Claw and Carlo and a few of Carlo's buddies — a black playwright name of Stud Jacks, a young Barone, a middle-aged Frenchman who teaches math at Bologna and has a mistress in Florence — and some of the other students whom I suspect Pete has impressed into service. This ensemble is held together by its singleminded ferocity, the alternate captaincy of Carlo and Pete, and the master strategies of Mr. Jacks, embodied in the single imperative: cheat. They have not yet arranged a match but they are negotiating with some local church-sponsored teams. Meanwhile they practice every Saturday afternoon in a mudfield at the Cascine. They split into demiteams and try to cream each other. Already the Barone, Jacks, and one of the students have had to be hauled apart in debates over the more exquisite points of the game; and the Frenchman has twice promised to emasculate Carlo. "We're shaping up," reports Pete, rubbing his bleeding paws together. "We're turning into a real team."

Mavis: 'Scuse me. Those're *my* cakes you're eating.

Goatee: So whattayou so threatened? That's my tea you been sloshing. Hey, Hatch, you made up your mind yet about coming with us to Venice?

Mavis: Venice. That tourist trap. Sascha, *carino, mangia la tua dolce.*

Sandra: Oh what a darling little boy. Yeah, Pete, come with us to Venice.

Pete (looking up from the *Nazione*): How much does it cost? Tourist traps're expensive. Hey — Florence is playing Pisa this weekend. You wanna go, Langer?

Langer: They playing here or Pisa? Now I had two rice cakes here — Jesus, the kid ate them. Hey. Kid. Sascha. You wanna be on our soccer team?

Pete: Pisa. How much does the bus to Pisa cost?

Goatee: Pisa, listen, you don't wanna go to Pisa for some stupid soccer game. Now Venice, they've got Art and stuff. Gondolas. You don't wanna go back without riding in a gondola, do you?

Mavis: Gondola in winter, wonkiest thing I ever heard of. I say, d'you want the rest of that tea?

Langer: That's what we need, a Russian on our team. Give us a little more weight. How about that, Claw? You — Sascha — good soccer team, OK?

Claw: Ya, ya, ya! Soccer! *Famos!*

Goatee: Jesus, stuff another cake in him before he knocks

somebody out. Listen, Hatch, yes or no with Venice. I've
gotta get the tickets

Pete: La chiesa accetta — I don't believe it. Read this. Maybe
I'm not translating right.

Arabella: La chiesa accetta la pillola. Good heavens. The
Church accepts the Pill . . . ?

(stunned silence)

Pete: Listen. Do you know what that means? We're getting
there. We're gonna *make* it. We get right down to the
wire and we're *rational.* We're gonna

Arabella: Wait. I — 'll translate the rest of the item. ". . .
Fra Giovanni, radical theologian, calls again for the church
to reverse its stand or suffer weakening of its pastoral
authority. He calls for a reexamination . . ."

Mavis: I *knew* it was a trick. Those dirty Catholics.

With nothing else to offer, I order another round of rice
cakes. If we keep their bellies full, maybe the kids won't
notice they're being screwed.

Child's Guide cont'd: The Uffizi, Room XII

Rinsing our palates on the Flemish, the great triptych of
Van der Goes. The Babe — deposited naked and partially
transparent, plunk in the middle of the world's trappings
of jewel-stiff robes, peacock feathers, ambereyed serpent —
is so recently born he lies there stunned, still trembling with
heaven's light, with having just that moment been set down
on earth.

From Pete, a groan. I don't need to look at his face to translate it: the groan has been wrenched from a rupture of disbelief. I move on through to the da Vincis, leaving him to seal up the hole as best he can. Or to cope with the awesome possibility of surrendering the rational.

The Uffizi, Room X

Sneaking back to the big Botticellis, the ones we missed when the guard booted us out. Pete contemplates the curved, longarmed ladies of the *Primavera*. "Now that is what I would call female," he pronounces.

Moving to the *Venus:* he stands a very long time. Transfixed; processing. Presently he sighs. "Women. My God. That Sandro, he knew them, didn't he?"

The Uffizi, West Loggia

"Pete, it's almost closing time. I really think we ought to go." The sweetness of the Botticellis have strangely curdled in my stomach.

"Wait . . . Wait."

He has stopped between the huge statues from the realistic school of Pergamus: Marsyas flayed and hanging by the wrists. The marble head stares down, obscenely grinning. "My God." Locked into the terrible marble eyes. "Why is he laughing?"

"The *risus sardonicus,* grin of death. Come on."

"Does something happen to the . . . muscles, or something?"

"I thought you didn't want to be instructed." (No longer a question of instruction but of belief: Marsyas's grin is recognition. *So it was a joke after all*.) "Pete, we have to go. We really have to go."

Piazza Signoria

— It's only three o'clock. I thought you said it was closing time. How about nipping over to the Bargello?

— Just an hour, Pete, I don't think

— An hour's an hour, we don't want to waste it. You're not getting tired, are you?

— Certainly not. It's just that

— *Brava*. She's got the endurance if not the weight. C'mon.

Bargello

Donatello's *David,* first nude statue of the Renaissance. He eases around it, methodically measuring (what does he see? the nudity enhanced by the broadbrimmed hat; the artist's tenderness for the girlish fanny; the knowing cock of knee, cant of pelvis?); then frowns, shakes his head, lopes away.

"What's in here?" Following me from the great salon he veers. "Nothing." "Nothing? A whole big room —" "Nothing interesting. Cases of old coins, silver, trinkets —" But he is methodical; he does not waste. He makes his way from case to case, bending to peer through the glass. I stand in the doorway rewrapping my coat across my chest. It is cold, very cold in this old stonepile, the stonedeep cold of places that have once been prisons.

"Hey. C'mere." He beckons me. "Look at these."

"I've seen them."

He bends to peer through the glass; case filled with little bronze figurines, sculptures of animals and humans in obscene positions; a bronze Leda copulating with a swan, a two-cock man suckling a giraffe with three breasts, a maiden mounted by a serpent-tailed bull —

A sudden clang on clang of metal; they're shutting the gates; it is closing time, they will close us in, we'll be locked in, imprisoned. Late, late! I turn tail and flee for the gates.

Huh. *Huh.* HUH. He catches up with me crossing the piazza. Grabs my elbow. "You split. Why?"

Young, young: translucent skin like a baby's pulled taut over bones so recently hardened; translucent blue gaze mild as a baby's, just now hardening in cold rationality. "It was closing time, Pete. I told you it was closing time. I didn't much care to be locked in there."

"You know they don't lock you in. They check." He drops his hand from my elbow. Stands regarding me. "Something's the matter. What?"

"I didn't want to be locked in."

He takes a deep breath. "Listen. All afternoon you've hardly said a word. Not even a comment on the Art —"

"You don't need comment anymore. You don't need instruction."

"Comment doesn't have to be instructive. Do you mind if we don't go over that again?"

"And do you mind if we don't stand here in the middle of the cold piazza arguing?"

He takes my elbow again, escorts me firmly over to the Loggia and up the steps and settles me down under the *Rape of the Sabines.* "I want to know what the matter is. I mean if I've offended you somehow, I oughtta know. Jesus. You're the last person I'd want to offend. I mean —"

"Offend, don't be silly." I rummage briskly in my purse for a cigarette. "You're making something out of absolutely nothing."

"Nothing," he repeats bleakly. "Maybe I've been sorta brash —"

"Brash, my goodness, you seem to think I'm not used to young people. Damn, I'm out of matches again."

"Young people. I suppose that's it. There must be a lot more interesting things you could be doing than trailing around museums with some" — a raw edge roughens his voice — "punk kid."

"Now don't start that again, grumping about kids not being people." I stand up briskly. My purse falls to the stone floor. He goes down on one knee to scoop up the scattered contents. His bent neck is long, assailable as a baby's. "Would I spend so much time with kids if I didn't consider you people, for heaven's sake? Since you mention it, though, I suppose I really ought to start spending a little more time on my work."

"Here's your matches." He slaps them into my palm, rises, hands me my purse. "Work? Jesus. I've been keeping you away from your work?"

"Not *you*. Not really, I mean. I've been sort of, well, stuck, blocked you might say, have been ever since I arrived . . . Any excuse," I add smiling brightly, "to goof off."

"Goof off? Is that what you figure we've been —"

"Not we, *me*. Heavens, Pete, I'm a grown woman, it's nobody's fault but my own I've been so lazy. I mean at *my* age I certainly know what my responsibilities are," and I smile wryly, briskly, "and they of course are in my work, which I simply must get back to, my goodness, here it is almost December and I hoped to have been well into it by the end of the semester — that's just before Christmas, you know —"

"I know. Jesus, don't you think I know when the end of the semester is?"

"— so you see I really *must* get to it, and let you tour away on your own now, OK?"

"It'll have to be." His voice is so young that I am filled with the most unexpected sense of sorrow; patting his arm and smiling and excusing myself I hurry off. Feel his gaze on my back as he stands alone in the cold wind of the piazza.

Must get to work. Can't keep goofing off. Procrastination — Mama always said — is the thief of time.

5 winter

Ugo's room is off the front hall, its door hidden by a curtain. A glimpse while Lina is cleaning: Ugo's room has no windows, only a small skylight which can be cranked open a few inches by a long metal rod. It is sparely furnished with a narrow bed, a chest of drawers, a naked lightbulb, and a large tinted photo of Domi the poodle in a silver frame. But in every corner there are stacks — bound neatly with twine and piled high as a man's head — of back issues of the Nazione.

Closeted in my room I labor diligently, sweeping up little piles of lint for my journal. Perhaps, after I have enough pages to stack and bind neatly with twine, I shall be able to compute the Question: Is history composed of lint piles?

Children, too, work at childish games. It seems that in soccer practice Carlo's right knee came in contact with Pete's right shoulder. Carlo is in the hospital.

I've been patronizing a new tearoom of late — the childish babble wearied me — but Pete and Langer have ferreted me out with this emergency news. They have just come from the hospital where Carlo is lying trussed in plaster on a bed of intensest Italian agony.

"I swear — I swear I didn't mean to do it." Pete holds his hands out from his body as if they were contaminated, gives them a shake as if to shake off drops of blood. "I was crouching to block him and he just kept coming. He's fast — you know how light he is" — a groan; another shake of the bloodied hands — "he just kept coming at top speed. He was planning to cut out around me, figured I couldn't move that fast. I had to. You gotta *move*. It's instinct. It's all reaction, you know?"

"Reaction," affirms Langer. "That's the name of the game."

"— so he cut and I moved. He must have turned two loops going over my shoulder. I could hear that tendon scream. I could feel it. Jesus."

"You did a neat job on him all right. Too bad it wasn't a bone instead of a tendon. Bones heal," says the doctor's son.

A series of awful groans from the Boston Mangler, who drops his head into his paws. "Poor old Carlo," Langer muses. "It'll probably take him forever to get on his feet."

"Carlo *is* pretty old." I fold my *Nazione,* rise, throw some lire on the table. "Well into his thirties. They may have to shoot him, like a horse." To the Mangler: "However, you might take comfort from the fact that if Carlo's that old he's old enough to know what to expect when he plays games with kids." I snap my purse closed.

"*Jesus.* What's the matter with her?" I hear Langer mutter as I depart. "Lately she's a regular witch."

"I'll be go to hell if I know," says Pete bleakly. "Maybe

she's having a hassle with her work. We oughtta be more patient with her, Langer."

The Nazione *carries a picture of the young Greek king Constantine and his wife getting off the plane to exile in Rome. "Poor little wife, poor little babies," mourns the old Signora rolling up her eyeballs. "Una famiglia proprio devastata, proprio tragica." And Greece? Shall we squeeze out a tear for it?*

Natalie Poirer and Seth Greene and one of the American hippies, a kid named Steve something, have been arrested and locked up in the Florence jail. The charge is possession of marijuana. It is a serious one.

"I told you, the Italians are medieval about this kind of thing." Maggi Miller, her skinny frame spread exhaustedly on the Greenes' couch, has swooped in with comfort and counsel. "The Americans are hung *up* of course but these people are beyond be*lief*."

"Belief we don't *POP* worry, what we have to worry is *SNAP* action." Eleanor, wigless and lashless and wearing a pair of tight pink stretch pants, bounces around the room looking with her cropped hair like a kewpie schoolboy. "Morty, never mind passing the peanuts, *POP*, try getting the Consul again, say it's an emergency."

"E*mer*gency, if you think *they* care," snorts Maggi, "you could be *dy*ing, the Italian phone system is fucked up beyond credi*bil*ity. I mean if you think AT&*T* —"

"*Per favore,* operator," Morty is droning into the phone, "*per favore, è un, ah, emergenzia* —"

"Let Arabella do it, Morty, and you go see if Langer's

got the *SNAP* suitcase ready, be sure he puts in warm socks, it's prolly cold in that *POP* jail."

"Oh it's *cold* all right, it's absolutely medieval —"

"Go home, Maggi," Eleanor Greene says evenly. "Go all the way home to Beverly Hills, why don't you, so you can *SNAP* bitch in civilized comfort."

After four days of fruitless negotiation Nat and Seth and the other boy are abruptly sprung.

The authorities came late at night to the Greene villa and after certain delicate arrangements had been effected — the transfer of the doctor's Mercedes to the Chief Inspector as a "goodwill gesture"; the signing of an inscrutable document turning over the "legal responsibility for any future eventuality rising from the release of the three prisoners" to Dr. Greene — said three prisoners were delivered out of the dark, from the Chief Inspector's private car in which they had been stashed, waiting. The Chief Inspector drove off in the Mercedes.

The reason for the sudden release became immediately clear: the Italian authorities didn't want the embarrassment of an American death on their hands. Steve, the hippie boy, was found to be comatose with an overdose of heroin which had, Seth said, been smuggled to him by a jail guard in exchange for Steve's guitar.

Despite Mort Greene's efforts the boy died on the couch a half-hour later. Nobody knows his last name. One of the kids on the Ponte Vecchio says he thinks Steve was from Cleveland, but he's not sure. "Maybe it was his sister he mentioned once, lived in Cleveland," the kid says.

Forty days and forty nights: that is what a week of rain seems, and now a mean bitter wind comes to lash it. And rooms are mean and bitter; I roam the city and it closes in on me like rooms, like time; like age. Did I believe that age, like death, would ever really arrive? After what seems like a mere forty days and forty nights, forty years will flood over me.

On the steps of the Loggia where I have paused a moment to get out of the wind, a hippie girl comes up to me and begs a cigarette. I give her one and light it for her. Silently she slouches back into the shelter behind the Sabine statue where her pals are huddled (future Roman matrons, what great Empire are you planning to build with the sons of your loins?). They confer; another girl detaches herself and slopes over to stand in front of me with her pelvis and her palm thrust out. I silently shake out another cigarette and lay it in her palm. She remains there, holding out the hand. "Yes?" I make it a question. She mutters, "You know, like, there's about eight of us." I flick my eyes over her. Her filthy hair half-hides her face; her jeans are split at the side; she has a thin torn battle jacket safety-pinned over her chest, a pigeon feather stuck in the lapel. Her lips are blue. There are blue hollows under her cheekbones. Her palm is bluish, waxy, flat, unlined. She regards me with flat eyes. I look down at her palm. I say, "Do we *owe* this to you?"

I open my hand. The pack of cigarettes drops to the Loggia steps.

The kids are starting to worry about finals, a couple of weeks away. I give no exam, I tell them. They reward me with relieved cheers.

Pete, silent and rockbound, remains in his chair at the foot of the table. I busy myself with papers; finally am forced to look up.

"Yes? Some question?"

"Yes. Some question." The silence falls again like a rock into the troubled moatblue gaze.

"Well?" I smile a schoolmarm smile.

He shovels up his books, stands wearily. "Nothing," he says, and lopes out.

Forty days and forty nights — it *seems* — and now perhaps the Flood? In the city an ancient unease reawakens. The citizens gather on the old bridge, gauging the enemy Arno. It has begun to boil, a baleful coffee-brown churning with debris, percolating up on angry chops. It slowly, hour by hour, climbs the sides of its trough. It is expected to crest at midnight. I scurry back out into the drenching dark, join the crowds down Borgo San Jacopo. The rain comes down with eerie efficiency, a baleful, almost palpable sense of purpose. Turning onto the Ponte Vecchio I draw in my breath. Unmistakable: the metabolic stink of the river, thrown on its furious spray.

In the open center of the span the silent citizenry keeps vigil. Flashlights play along the great pontoons. The river humps against them like a demented animal, upending logs, ramming and lunging. Its breath here is choking. The old bridge shudders beneath our feet. Unimaginable, the force that could shake this huge stony span. I remember, with a sudden shiver, the legend: the city will survive only as long as the Old Bridge endures. Thinking of the enormous surface it presents to the water — rigid, an ungiving wall with absolutely no allowance for negotiation — I sense the stubborn resistance of superstition, holding out for countless centuries against the steady battering of reason. When it cracks, all history will be swept away.

"He cometh to bring us salvation, so there's no call to worry," chimes the familiar voice above the crashing of the waters, the gnashing of the storm, the mutter of the populace; and the wraithlike figure of the Campanile is borne past among the throng, head and shoulders high like some sacred statue of the Madonna.

I push across to the Lungarno, where floodlights illuminate a swarm of workers piling sandbags onto the half-finished structure of the new wall, started after last year's devastation. The boardwalk is afloat in a wallow of mud, choked with shopkeepers carting away their merchandise in bags, baskets, wheelbarrows, on backs. The little new shops are bright-lit, gutted of all but their gleaming tile, their handsome new fixtures. A stout middleaged proprietress is struggling to wheel a cartload of white plaster *Davids* away to safety; her barrow has been forced off the walk and she's trying to hoist it back out of the mire. Her high-heeled shoes have foundered, her elegant pompadour has fallen over her face.

Permesso. Somebody trying to pass me on the walkway while I'm trying to back up. "Lady, please —" Unmistakably American, unmistakably Boston, unmistakably "Pete?" "Yeah." He swings me around him and plunges across the walkway. *"Permesso,"* he says, grabbing the wheel of the proprietress's barrow and heaving. She lets go the handles and begins to pommel his back with her fists. *"Va via,"* she screams, her face in the floodlight wild through her streaming hair, *"va via, turisto! Via, via, americano!"* Under the rain of fists Pete gives a final mighty heave and the barrow is lifted from the mud and its wheel set back on the walkway. *"Via, via, via!"* the woman screams after him as he lurches back.

"I shoulda known." We stand on the Santa Trinità bridge looking back up the humping torrent, humping our shoulders under our drenched coats; "I shoulda known."

"She was panicked," I say. "People aren't rational when they're panicked."

"Oh I know that. What I mean, I shoulda known better than to come out in a pair of clean pants. Look at the mud." He lifts a knee. "Damn."

"Is that blood you've got all over yourself too?"

"Damn." He lifts his hands; blood trickles from palms down both wrists. "I s'pose it was that cable . . . Do you know how much they charge you to launder a pair of pants? Three hundred lire. Almost fifty cents. *Damn.*"

By morning the crisis is over. The rain slackens, the waters begin to recede. The *Nazione* reports that the river crested at such-and-such meters and that the weather outlook is for showers diminishing tomorrow to very cold. The entire front page is given over to an editorial praising the Mayor, whose quick thinking and bravery have, it appears, saved the city.

" 'S'not good, you know."

"What's not good?"

"Moping." Mavis thrusts out her lower lip in the bullying way I have come to recognize as her means of hiding the tenderer sentiments, which she calls "soppy." She leans against my door as if bracing it up. "Hiding yourself away behind your so-called work. Won't solve it, you know."

"Solve what, for heaven's sake. Really, Mavis —"

"Whatever it is," she says darkly, "that needs solving. Won't work. Oh close the door if you want, I'm used to being shut out, one can't take offense at every petty insult if one's going to make one's mark. Taking offense, moping and brooding, *that* sort of thing doesn't get one far. I shall simply invite somebody else to the lecture. Can't waste a ticket one's paid good money for."

The British Institute Lecture Series, I see, is patronized mostly by old ladies in purple toques. As soon as we sit Mavis leans forward, taps the old lady in front, and tells her to remove her hat. "One can't *see*," she hisses as the old lady turns to attack; and in the exchange of glares the old lady — recognizing perhaps that mark of Eminent Domain so implicit in British rudeness — backs down and removes her toque. One has to admire Mavis's adaptive perfection, the way one admires the giraffe's neck, the cactus, the shark.

> *Water, water everywhere,*
> *Nor any drop to drink.*

"Hideously true," yawns Mavis, checking her watch. " 'Ancient Mariner' indeed. — I say, what's the matter with *you?* You look as if you'd seen a ghost."

Up on the podium the plankless specter's old face is bare
and hungry as an ox skull. But flash of the bluest blue,
hypnotic as memory itself, in the sockets sweeping the hall;
the old fist hoists dramatically, the black Victorian poet's
cape swirls —

"Shhh, I'm OK," I murmur. "I *have* seen a ghost."

"Great Scott, you have? Where?"

"Up there. The . . . speaker. Timothy Sandys."

"Doesn't look like a ghost to *me*," snorts Mavis indig-
nantly. "Though he's probably *old* enough —"

"Shhh." The old lady has turned, glaring elaborately.
"Old friend," I whisper. "Tell you about it later."

*Truly historic: Timothy Sandys sheds the historic light of grace.
It strengthens with the length of his survival; ragged old-man's
spareness, huge flat widehipped old frame, long old shanks flat as
slats, long old-man's earlobes, long yellow-gray lank hair cut in
the Dutch manner of the Victorian poets of whom he is surely
the last survivor. A grandeur still, even in his tattered clothes,
threadbare tweeds, declamatory old Victorian cape. But it is his
countenance — bony, grottoed, ruddy, long and broad of chin
and cheekbone and brow, expansive of nose, bursting of vein,
blue of eye — which casts back the beauty of the Lord's light. It
is dazzling, that light; his eyes have the sunblasted look of a
man who has stared full into the face of the Lord.*

"My dear girl. Oh this is lovely, lovely. Can it really be
you? Or is it more apposite to ask if it's really me . . .
Dinner, oh how perfectly delightful of you. Was going to
mush back home on the seven o'clock bus to Arezzo but
since you're going to feed me . . .

"My dear mmmmm Arabella how very posh. Such a splendid restaurant. In the country one leads such a simplified life. Now then dear girl let's look at you. My word. Twenty years. Barely dented you. Astounding.

"Now tell me what you've been up to, since — drat, I get these gaps, sometimes remember things simply decades ago and sometimes haven't the foggiest — ah! You were a student at dear Mercedes's, we used to have some splendid chats when I came to tea, I remember, and oh yes, yes, Mercedes brought you young ladies down to the farm once or twice, I remember, in the spring, to see the daffodils . . . Dear Mercedes, she corked off, y'know, shortly after you left, was it '49? '48. Terribly young, Mercedes, in her fifties I b'lieve. Pneumonia. Whisked her off. Her school closed immediately, of course, too bad, tsk, no place left here now for a young lady to come and get a proper finishing, literary education I mean, Keats and Shelley and so on. But dear me, mustn't dwell on the past, must we . . .

"Oh dear here I've eaten all the cheese. Afraid I'm as greedy as ever. However. Still chugging along. One survives. S'prising how little things change. The olives have done famously this year — and the honey, of course. The vines somewhat less with all this bloody rain. What with one thing and another, like tonight's reading at the Institute — one manages. Had rather planned if the vines did well to go back to England for a bit of a holiday this coming summer. M'grandnevvew's being married and it's been eight years — no, by George, this is '67 now, isn't it — nine years since I've seen m'sister. Marvelous old girl, used to be an actress, y'know. Her Desdemona was superb. But then this plagued rain. Oh well. *Niente da fare.* P'raps next year . . .

"Oh dear here I've been chattering along — one does chatter frightfully — and I haven't pried a syllable out of you about yourself. But I s'pect you don't really want to, do you? Talk about yourself, I mean. Some sadness I think, something recent . . . Although what people consider recent, makes no difference how far back it was, does it? No such thing as an end to mourning, really, is there? Like saying Oh this missing leg? it was amputated years ago, I'm not crippled anymore. Well, I won't ask, no good asking, only good telling — when one wants to, of course . . .

"No no dear mmmmmm Arabella couldn't cram down another bite, here it is eight-thirty and at nine sharp I must pick up the last Arezzo bus. Always best to sleep in one's own bed, y'know. You're here for a while, I b'lieve you said? Lovely. Splendid. What you must do, my dear, you must come down and spend a few days at the farmhouse. 'Twill have to be after New Year's, I'm making a small retreat till then, Anglican monastery over near Urbino, they've a simply splendid table, no use chastising ancient flesh, time's done enough of that. Well, all those old chaps at the Retreat, one will be quite ready to see a young face by then. So you simply must come, my dear mmmmm Arabella, act of charity y'know. Twenty years, my word, since you were last there with dear Mercedes. I s'pect a great deal more's happened to you than to me. But one survives, doesn't one? Yes. Tsk. One survives, in the gracious light of the Lord's countenance. Ah how rich is life, and full of small explosions."

—You could've invited *me* along to dinner. After all, it started out to be *my* treat.

— Dear Mavis. Forgive me. I didn't mean to abandon you. It was such a shock, an old friend I'd thought was dead. Dear old friend, really. Dear old man.

—Well . . . It must've done you *some* good. You seem to've quit moping. You see I was right, of course.

Carlo is out of the hospital, just in time to host the Ferinis' semiannual catchall social bash marking the semester's end.

Attending: American Consul & Wife; contingents & wives of I Tatti and Fulbrights and art historians and sabbatical scholars; Headmaster of St. John's Episcopal Day School; resident gung-ho American Novelist & Wife; some sere old crusts of the British Colony; the soccer-squad Barone; a widowed Marchese (Bryn Mawr '29); selected students including the Mangler who is drawing admiration for his handiwork (Carlo is limping picturesquely with the aid of a cane); Stud Jacks the black playwright; Maggi Miller (who knows *every*body); the Greenes; and Carlo's father, a handsome old ranking *maestro* (I understand that up until the War and the Occupation and his activities in the Resistance, *maestro* Ferini was one of Italy's most promising violinists. German interrogators chopped off the two middle fingers of his left hand trying to get to the Question).

Refreshments: martinis and chocolate eclairs.

Student #1: gotta leave next week and there's all these things I was gonna do. I never even got up to Fiesole, never went inside the Medici Palace.

Student #2: supposed to come back speaking fluent Italian, I got bogged down in the *passato remoto*

Student #3: I got bogged down with Angelina, she's one of those gigglers, every time I

Student #4: never watched the sun come up over piazzale Mich after a mad night of love

Student #1: all I've got to show for it is my 127 postcards of the Art Treasures of the

Maggi: followed me all the way down via Tornabuoni, *if* you can imagine. They think American women find them irresistible, my gawd, it's the fault of these middleaged American matrons, they just *die* for the Italian boys

British Crust: Eh. Hrmmph. Quite.

Maggi: I mean everywhere you *turn* there's some raddled old American bitch, hips out to *here,* hanging on the arm of some sixteen-year-old *ragazzo.* If they only knew how pa*the*tic they

Cassandra: Major Burke-Henning, hi. Can I get you a martini?

B.C.: Thenk-you m'dear. Pierino's fetching m'one.

Cassandra: Pierino? Oh yeah, your protégé.

Maggi: I don't see how any woman with any self-res*pect* can take an Italian man *ser*iously. Cassie darling these martinis are fantastic. Oh gawd it's so good to have someone hand you a *prop*er martini

Barone: Eeeeh Pietro, pieno pietra! Come stai, amico? Ecco il detrito, povero Carlo, zoppo dalla gamba!

Pete: Thanks. I wouldn't blame you if this martini were poisoned, Carlo. How's it, uh, feel?

Carlo: Shitty. I live on aspirin. Such pain. *Senti,* have you arranged a match?

Barone: Impossibile. Tutti hanno sentito del' nostro Devastatore famoso. Tutti hanno paura —

Pete: Scared. Of me? Jesus. Listen, you know I'm leaving next week, you guys'll have to find somebody to take my place.

Carlo: Impossibile. Senti, there is a Lucca team just formed, full of peasants and butchers

Eleanor: Nat's in France somewhere, she won't go home, there's evidently a lotta *POP* hostility there with her parents over the drug scene, looks like they sent her over here to get her away from it. Some of these parents think the solution's shipping the kids away from the scene, they don't *SNAP* realize the youth scene's pretty much the same everywhere, cuts through cultures, an American *POP* kid is more like a French or a German kid than he is like his *SNAP* parents. A new subculture

Arabella: Seth? How's he doing?

Eleanor: He's in Switzerland. The lawyer advised us to get him out of the *POP* country for a while.

Arabella: I thought *they* were the ones who were so anxious to drop the whole thing?

Eleanor: Oh the local authorities, definitely. But evidently Steve's parents are making some *SNAP* fuss through the embassy in Rome, threatening an investigation. God knows I . . . can't blame them

Arabella: Eleanor. You can't blame yourselves, you and Mort, for

Eleanor: We're all to blame and you know it. All us parents and *POP* teachers, our generation — no Morty we don't want an eclair — somehow we've managed to fuck it up and fail them, failed to provide, given them *SNAP* Art and orthodonture and the Pill and a New Ethic and counseling and it all turns out to be so much *POP* baling-wire

Headmaster: New Math textbooks, it's utter *devastazione* trying to get an order through from Rome

Mrs. Sabbatical: all very well for Language and Art but what're the kiddos going to do when they get back to San Jose which has a very strong emphasis on the Science program and they've missed an entire year, I mean it's hard enough getting into a decent college, I don't see how a kiddo can miss a whole year and expect to compete

Mrs. Fulbright: morning Chapel, it's confusing to kids who aren't Episcopalians, my Becky came home the other day practically bawling, she wanted to know how come *we* don't love Baby Jesus

Headmaster: just feel we *do* lean over backwards to be ecumenical

Marchese: Sandys . . . Tim? Did you hear that, Tony? Mrs. Sutherland says she ran into Tim Sandys the other day. She's an old friend of his.

Maestro Ferini: And then of course of ours.

Marchese: Dear old Timmie. My grief, it's been years. High old times we used to have. He gave the gayest parties. Remember, Tony, we used to all drive down to the farmhouse for his Sunday soirées, before the

Maestro Ferini: My dear Edith, you must persuade Signora
Sutherland to join us for bridge. We need a fresh young
face, no?

Marchese: You probably do, Tony. Yes, join us for bridge
next Tuesday. My chauffeur can pick you up if you want.
By the way, the stakes are a hundred lire a point.

Maestro Ferini: Should she also be warned that we cheat?
As one grows older, Signora, one becomes impoverished
for ways to raise the pulse rate. But of course you will not
understand this for many years yet.

Maggi: never thought I'd see the day when Eleanor Greene
turned *maso*chist. Do you realize they've turned that villa
into a crisis center, a *crash* pad for any kid who wanders
in? I mean she's developed this *guilt* complex. It's so
weirdly Prot-*Eth*.

Novelist: Well, they're Jewish. That clue you?

Maggi: Gawd. I *think* I see what you mean. Mmmm. I
think I see what you *mean*.

Mrs. Novelist: Sam says it's the reluctance to abandon linearity that's destroying the genre. Isn't that right, honey?
Sam says the novelist has to come to grips with the *objet
trouvé*

Novelist: vérité, Sylvia. Cinéma vérité. In terms of the visual

Art Historian: Punto. Empirical. After all it's the extraction
of emotional content, Art as the *act*

Mrs. Art Historian: waited in Venice six weeks for the light
to hit the frescoes just right, didn't we, honey? Jack says
subjective response is the only valid evaluative

Stud Jacks: shitty bag, putting a joe or two on the moon. Billions of bucks for the space race while brothers die in the ghetto. This crap about man's dream. This reaching-the-stars shit. I say fuck the dream. Fuck the stars. I say let us talk about stomachs. Let us discuss bread.

Arabella: Let us say man lives by bread alone?

Stud Jacks: Looks like you never had much worryin over bread, doll. Looks like you affordin fancy shit like dreams.

Arabella: Your last play's a big success — a parable on the nature of man, didn't I read, set in a subway toilet? Did you write it because you're an artist with a dream, or did you write it for the bread?

Stud Jacks: What you gettin at, baby? Tryin to get at me on account of my art brings me bread?

Arabella: That may bother you, baby, but it bothers me hardly at all you got paid well. I don't mind taking money for my own work. The crass old system of effort and reward seems to be built into the species, so let's recognize it and adjust it to make it fair so we can live with it, OK? What I'm getting at is that the need not just to eat but to dream seems to be built in too. Or are you really persuaded that all man's hunger resides in his belly?

Maggi: Hey. I know *you*. You're Goliath. You're the giant who slew poor little David. You're the *foot*ball player. Gawd, I thought football players went out with *di*nosaurs.

Sabbatical: Tyrannosaurus, wasn't it?

Maggi: No, *di*nosaurs were the ones with the teentsy brains. *Look* at you. You oughtta be a*sha*med, great big guy like

you, picking onna poor weak Italian. Hey. C'mon back
here. Lemme feel your muscle.

Sabbatical: Watch out. He looks hostile.

Maggi: Lemme feel your *mus*cle, I said. Gawd. Omigawd
feel this. Mort — Cassie — come and *feel* this brute's *mus*-
cle. Stud sweetie, come *here* and

Consul: complaints about this Woodcock girl. There's been
some awkward situations. The police keep bringing her
around to us, depositing her on our doorstep as if we were
an orphanage.

Eleanor: You mean they keep *SNAP* arresting her? She's
not doing anything wrong. She's just a little *SNAP*
crazy.

Pete: I don't think she's really crazy, Mrs. Greene. Maybe
sort of a linthead.

Eleanor: Well, fixated, she certainly has this *POP* father
fixation. Or maybe Jesus Christ's a brother figure? I
oughtta ask somebody *POP* Episcopal. Arabella? Listen, do you see Jesus as more of a brother or a father

Consul: They don't arrest her, of course. She doesn't do
anything illegal, she just keeps precipitating small incidents.

Pete: Yeah, she does do that.

Consul: For instance the other night she was up at the convent of the Sisters of Divine Mercy, passing out those
pamphlets of hers. Mind you, a Catholic convent —

Eleanor: *they* see Him as husband, of course. I mean there's
your classical case of *SNAP* sublimation

Consul: considerable upset. The Mother Superior called us. She didn't want to call the police, she likes the girl

Pete: She's a nice girl.

Consul: The Mother Superior calls her *La Santa Pazza.* Holy Madwoman.

Eleanor: very classical, saintliness and madness exhibit similar clinical dysfunction syndromes, every culture has its

Consul: Doubtless; and they're always an embarrassment. How do you deal with these people? Frankly we're worried that someday she's going to precipitate a really embarrassing

Pete: Historical precedent is if you can't cure 'em you kill 'em.

Consul: Oh come now, young man. We're a little more civilized than that.

Pete: Sir, the Vietnamese are an embarrassment. And our asylums and prisons are still full of people whose main problem, when you get right down to it, is that they're an embarrassment.

Old British Crust #1: God save our gracious Queen,

O.B.C. #2: Long live our noble Queen,

O.B.C. #3: Long may she reign.

Headmaster: Send her victorious,

Maggi: Happy and glorious

Pete: Can I get you another martini?

Arabella: I'm not finished with this one.

Pete: Listen. I heard what that guy was saying to you awhile ago. I want to say that

Arabella: We're hearing all sorts of things tonight, sonny. What guy?

Pete: The playwright. He was giving you a pretty rough time, and I want to

Arabella: Rescue me? Gallant of you, sonny, but I hardly think I'm in need of

Pete: say I agree with you. About the moon-shot I mean. Not as an international competition or a race to get there first — and personally I don't know enough about science to be curious about what they'll find. And of course anybody in his right mind knows we've gotta do something and do it right now about what he was saying — the bread thing, poverty, blacks, inequality. We can't just talk.

Arabella: Oh we can talk all right. Oh how we can talk.

Pete: What I'm saying is your talk made sense to me. This, you know, reaching-for-the-stars stuff. The need to know. The *effort.* You were saying we've gotta hang onto it.

Arabella: Hang onto what?

Pete: What you were talking about. All of man's hunger not being in his stomach. The, uh, Impossible Dream, I guess.

Arabella: I see. The Impossible Dream. How very heartening, to find that such unabashed idealism still exists in the young — and the rational. You've got an A for the semester. Teachers are always so pathetically grateful when students grasp the Question.

Pete: That . . . better be the martini talking.

Arabella: *In martini veritas.* And from it one last bit of instruction, sonny. The difficulty is not so much that the dream is impossible, but the reality.

Pete: You got to try.

Arabella: Oh indeed yes. Except that reality's so *real,* isn't it?
Pete: You got to try.

And then sometimes you got to quit. When it is too late. Oh yes it is certainly late, and there is all this stuff I've filled my belly with quite inadvertently, but that is the story of history is it not, people getting a bellyful of one thing and another. So goodbye everybody, lovely party, goodbye beautiful Cassandra always expecting bad news and goodbye Carlo, *grazie molto,* glad they didn't have to shoot you, and you've learned never to play games with kids because you will get

Ambushed? But it is only fresh air, winier than cold greenwhite wine from stonecold crocks. Crocked and stonecold Arabella out here on the piazza under the stonecold night shot through with brilliants. Fine night for shooting down the stars, for

Ambush! Out of the shadows of the piazza a dark form breaks, lurches toward me. Omigod. I whirl my whirling head: darkness, emptiness, silence; only me, alone in the middle of the piazza. He is coming up fast, like an express train. No use screaming; save your breath; *run.*

Huh *Huh* HUH my own breath chugging like an express train in my ears and *OOF.* Omigod he caught me. Omigod I won't be caught, I won't be raped, I won't be

"Stop —" trapped; I heave myself loose with an elbow jab, "You — *gghhh* —" dip cunningly and lunge up with a haymaker, boiling mad now, "forgot your *yike* —" with a karate chop HOH! HAH! to the "coat. *Arrrgggh.*"

Slowly he topples, with a crash like a mighty redwood.

Odear. Didn't mean to chop down our National Resources.

Slowly he hoists himself back up. Replants the great trunk, pokes the nose into my face and says in strangulated tones, "Next time check to see if it's one of your own team."

"Listen, sonny," I pant, "if you suspect rape you don't stop to check."

"Rape! Would I —"

"Rape old ladies, of course not," I say very dignified, as the block seems to have become recrocked, "although there are a lot of perverts in this world, even from Boston or perhaps I should say especially from Boston if one follows the newspapers."

"Put on your coat and stop badmouthing Boston," he snaps.

You don't have to walk me home. I am entirely ca-ba-ble.
Yeah.
Coach will be sore. Late hours
Yeah.
I am per-fect-ly safe. Italy is not a violent society. They still have the family and those mamas.
Yeah. Quit walking in the street.
But you limp. You lurch when you lope. Is it your football knee?
I limp when it's late. Get back on the sidewalk.
I lurch when it's late. See?
Get *all* the way back on the sidewalk.
But I want to see how it feels to have a valorous injury.
I never played football.

Women aren't supposed to play football.

Ethel does. Ethel plays a valorous game of football.

Ethel's a classy lady. But she just plays touch.

You dig the Kennedys, right?

I dig the Kennedys, right.

Camelot, right? The Impossible Dream, right?

Right. I'm not gonna argue it again. I'm not gonna argue it tonight and I'm not gonna argue it with you.

Who's arguing? This may come as a surprise to you, sonny, but you don't have the franchise on the Kennedys and Camelot and the Impossible Dream. Some of us elderly folks — quit grabbing my elbow, will you? You don't have to support me. I am not yet in my dotage. That starts tomorrow. December seventeenth is Dotage Day

Yeah, well, December eighteenth is Finito Day. That's when I — watch the curb — leave Florence. Listen, there's something I

can't, can not, ab-so-lutely can*not*. Never. Oh boo hoo hoo. Who'd have thought nevermore?

Jesus, what caused that? Hey. No sitting on the curb. This is no place to quit. What I was gonna say

Oh yes it is. This is the place, now is the hour. Oh late! Too late. I quit. Boo hoo. Who'd have thought I'd turn out to be a quitter? Dotage Day and it's all over

Dotage, that's ridiculous. Here, take this and wipe your face.

Can't wipe away the years, Oh boo hoo hoo. Forty years old and I've lost the Question and all the Answers

Yeah well I'm twenty years old and I haven't even found

a Question yet and never had any Answers and I'm not bawling about it. At least you know what to look for . . . C'mon. Please.

can't work anymore, can't even teach

Now that is ridiculous. You're a great teacher. You oughtta know that. You — Hell. You're in no condition to listen. We'll argue this later. C'mon. Up. It's too

late. Later, latest, too late. Tomorrow I'll be

Hung over. Wipe your face.

through.

Through, *SNORT*, that's the silliest thing I ever heard. Don't you ever look in the mirror? Come on now. Up. Let's get you home.

This is a cotton handkerchief. Didn't your mother tell you a gent carries linen handkerchiefs?

You're crazy. You know that? Sometimes you are really crazy. Anybody ever tell you that?

Yes, but he was wearing a tie with a pink flamingo painted on it. Would *you* believe a man who

C'mon, *pazza*. You got the guts

if not the weight. Right?

Right. Hang in. We're almost there. There's the bridge.

Finito Day

Preceded by *una notte bianca,* a white night, the Italians say of insomnia. I drifted through a white night in a cloud of whitened semidreams, unable to sink all the way down into sleep. The dreams were full of voices. I should resign myself, welcome them. When the sound of voices ceases the silence will commence.

Alone at my desk with the breakfast coffee old Agata has brought me I lean my head on my hand and gaze out the window at the sky. It is slowly turning from dawn gray to a peculiar colorless white. Even the stone wall of the cortile which usually strengthens in tint with the rising light remains inert, whitening. I light my cigarette and gaze dully out the dull window, where it has begun to look like

Snow? "Why, it's snowing," I murmur aloud. The flakes are sifting down slowly, scattering motes against the inert sky. Something arcs in me, fuses. It snowed the day I was born. Forty years ago Seattle had a great, rare blizzard. I lift my coffee cup in a toast. Happy birthday, then.

The doorbell peals, rupturing the Sunday-morning calm. Domi the poodle barks sharply, skitters down the hall, old Agata shuffling and muttering after. In a moment, a rap on my door.

Happy birthday! An explosion of young voices, a flowering of young faces.

> *We shall overcooooooome,*
> *We shall overcooooooome,*

Barrelling down the autostrada in the snow falling like a blessing, a birthday frosting.

"But how did you know? I didn't tell anybody —"

"Didn't tell, *SNORT*, never saw anybody put up such

an obvious fight." Pete, hunched over the wheel, scowls be-
nignly out into the blizzard. "It didn't have to snow, though.
We shoulda canceled the picnic."

"Cancel, rubbish, with all this food bought," sniffs Mavis.
"Bit of snow, can't stop *us*."

"When the going gets tough, the tough get going," says
Langer. "Hey, lookit the Fiats, all piled in the ditch."

"You look, I'm driving," says Pete grimly. "Sascha, quit
hanging on my elbow. It's tricky enough steering — *Sascha,
basta.*"

"*Stai securo, Sascha carino, Gesù ti guarda.* He's not used
to ridin in cars," chimes the Campanile who is folded serenely in the back seat. "It sure does beat walkin."

"You were planning to walk to San Gimignano?" Mavis
snorts.

"Is that where we're going, San Gimignano?" I hadn't
thought to ask. Tuscany in the snow. Tender plump white
clinging to the olives, filling the hedgerows, piling up
plumply over the vines. Who'd believe olives in the snow?

"Oh we weren't fixin to walk there today. Come spring
we're goin on a walkin mission, spread the Word down
round Siena, Rome."

"San Gimignano's Mavis's bright idea," Langer says. "She
wants to see the obscene frescoes in some church."

"We're driving through a raging blizzard to look at some
obscene frescoes?" Pete swerves savagely. "Jesus, did you see
that? These maniacs, haven't they ever seen snow before?"

"And medieval towers, y'know. Actually quite interesting.
The village is a national monument," lectures Mavis, "origi-

nal walls and all that, used to be a Roman outpost, prob'ly Etruscan before that—"

"So whattawe, picnic sitting on top of one of the towers?" Langer inquires. "Is that what you had in mind?"

"Couldn't we picnic in the fields? Everything's so beautiful," I say. "Look at that line of cypress, edged with snow over there against the hill—"

"Bully idea. We'll gather twigs and faggots—"

"Faggots, ew, are there many of those in this village? because oh fudge, I forgot to bring my ruffled dress—"

"—and build a roaring fire. Yes. Splendid."

"With wet wood?"

"Bit of snow never hurt anybody," says Mavis stoutly. "If it's too filthy we'll simply find a farmer's barn and build our fire in there."

"Oh groovy. A barn-fire."

"Listen, *ragazzi*," fumes Pete, "if this gets any worse we'll picnic in the car. I musta been outta my gourd—"

"Oh Pete quit grumping," I cry. "Look how beautiful everything is. Oh this must be the most beautiful birthday I ever had."

"Christmassy," agrees the Campanile. And she begins sweetly to chime

> *Joy to the world,*
> *The Lord is come!*

And the children chime in, sweetly singing, as we leave the autostrada and begin the climb up into the snowy Tuscan hills.

At the top of the hill, the end of the road: the walls of San Gimignano. A great plane of barrier stone disappearing up into muffled white. Our tire marks are the only break in the broad clearing of the *campo*. We spill out of the car. We stop, gawping with the sudden cold, the stillness which — after our riotous singing and laughter — has a holy smell.

"Man. It is so quiet." Our voices sound eerie in the silence. It is snowing so heavily we cannot see the top of the portals. We can only sense the walls' stone bulk, curving away into impenetrable white; sense their immense age and weight and persistence. Through the yawning arch we can discern, like a tunnel entrance, the beginning of a tiny narrow street. It slopes up like a white ramp between overhanging stone buildings before it too is swallowed up in white. "Jeez. Those walls must be fifty feet high."

"Well . . ." We stand looking at each other. We're a pretty motley crew: me in a pink felt hat, Langer in battle jacket and feathered green Alpine cap; the Campanile covered with a poncho that was once a plaid blanket; Mavis in red pompommed crocheted tam; little bear-cub Sascha all but engulfed by an enormous fur shako and what looks like a woman's muskrat shortie; surmounted by the blond summit of Mount Hatch, in his letterman's sweater with the big scarlet block H. "Well . . ."

"C'mon!" At the captain's command the motleys charge the portals. Hollering, scooping snow, the captain and Lieutenant Langer barrel through the archway, Sascha at their heels; sprint up the ramp, round a corner and are swallowed up.

"Well." The Ladies' Auxiliary, Mavis and the Campanile and I, start out after them.

The ramp climbs steeply. It is narrow, crooked, utterly deserted; a close winding warren. The ramshackle old stone buildings seem to lean over us as we climb, their tops muffled in dense white, their windows shuttered tight. The only sign of life: the boys' footprints in the snow. "I say, where're all the people?" puffs Mavis. "Indoors, I guess." "Ridiculous, bit of snow, can't venture out into it." The Campanile is floating along, humming softly to herself, pausing now and then to lay a pamphlet down in front of a snowsealed doorway. "Ladies," I urge, "a bit faster. We're losing the spoor." "Got to be a bloody mountain goat," pants Mavis, her face the color of her tam.

We climb faster, our feet scrabbling in the soft new snow. The alleyway has steepened. Presently Mavis stops. "This's the wrong way," she puffs. "There's no footprints." We've come out in a tiny piazza, a widening in the network of crooked alleys tunneling off at random. Except for a mound covering what looks like a well-pump the clearing is smooth, unbroken.

"Where'd they go?" complains Mavis. "I say, you chaps!" Her shout ruptures the stillness.

"Shhh," I say automatically, reaching out to touch her arm. At that moment my hat lifts from my head, spins across the clearing, hits a wall, flops.

The hat seems to have done this of its own volition, it was so swift and soundless. Not even the brush of a "Snowball," I mutter. I skitter across to retrieve my hat which is leaning against the wall of a building, half-buried in snow; as I bend I'm hit in the butt so jarringly that I'm thrust forward onto my hands and knees. At the same moment I hear Mavis grunt and fall. I go into a crouch with my arms over my head. The hit was so hard my spine feels paralyzed all the way up to my back teeth.

"It's not funny," Mavis whimpers after a moment. "Those filthy boys, playing tricks." Like me she is crouched in the snow, her fat face furious, her tam over one eye. She pulls it straight. "That really hurt, you little beasts!" she yells, shaking her fist and glaring around. "Pete — Langer — we saw you chaps! Come out, you cowardly —" Cowed by the ringing stillness, she stops. "Wait'll I catch the filthy little beasts," she mutters, hauling herself to her feet and brushing at her jacket. The Campanile seems to have floated off in another of her disappearing acts. Crouched by the wall I can see the pink rim of my hat sticking up out of the feathery whiteness. I reach over to pull it out. As the snow brushes away I see something underneath, mounded against the wall. I brush with my hat. It is a dead dog. Dried blood coats its fur in round craters. There is a pile of stones around it.

The stillness has thickened, like the beat of the snow, like wings brushing. I brush the snow back over the stiffened corpse. I pick myself up, dust off. Mavis's hand is cupped over her ear. When she removes it there is a clot of blood on her mitten. "Must've packed a stone in that snowball, monstrous little animals," she mutters.

"C'mon." Blindly choosing an alley we scrabble on, lurching and slipping. It is astonishing how naked I feel. The alley opens abruptly and we are at the top of the hill. A sudden dazzling expansion of light and white: a large piazza, commanded by a church. We halt, blinking.

"There they are! You filthy wretches, you're going to *pay* —" Beyond Mavis I catch a glimpse of a clot of bright color in the middle of the piazza and then we are mowed down.

The attack is paralyzing. It feels like a hail of bullets. We topple to our knees. Another burst; we are flattened. A sharp pain in my side. I double up, grunting. Someone — Mavis; Sascha? — screams. Another volley and I feel my hat torn off again and glimpse it flying; a large black form runs toward me and in my astonishing pain and struggle for breath I don't understand what happens except that somebody's hands are in my armpits hoisting me and my rib becomes a steel sliver twisting into my lung and I am grunting because there's no air for a scream; I'm half-run half-hauled over the snow and up some steps where I'm shoved into a doorway under the groin of some arch. Propped there and abandoned.

Muffled grunts, animal sounds nearby; farther out into the eerie stillness there is a noise like pigeons' wings, beating. I blink; the snow melts on my lashes. Through the water-lens I see vague moving forms down there in the center of the white. I blink again. I am huddled under the sheltering groin of the church doorway. Mavis and the Campanile are propped on either side of me, the fat girl huddled with her arms across her stomach. A trickle of blood runs from under her tam down her cheek into the corner of her mouth. Up above me the sunflower face is white except for a red welt high on the cheekbone which has swollen an eye closed and sealed it with a yellowblack glaze, its colorations like bugs against a windshield. The other eye is round and she is staring across to the far side of the piazza. There is a wall of buildings across there, a jumbled façade of blank windows and crumbling balconies and landings like balconies with outside staircases. On one of these landing balconies there seems to be movement, a shifting clotted dark form. I blink, shifting the watery lens. The balcony shifts into a clump of men. Bundled in thick dark overcoats they look like parts of a huge beetle that has crawled halfway up the wall. The antennae wave; I see arcs of brownish motes falling through the white snow down into the center of the piazza, onto a little clump of bright color.

I blink once more and my vision clears. Pete and Langer and Sascha are clumped together in the middle of the piazza, hurling snowballs up at the men on the balcony. The men on the balcony are lobbing stones. The balcony is piled high with stones; they rain down on the piazza with a sound like a thousand pigeons' wings beating.

As I watch, I catch a movement at the periphery of white. Another group of men is silently streaming from an alleyway into the piazza from behind the church. They stream noiselessly out like dark oil, swiftly and steadily spreading out onto the white until they are spread below us at the foot of the cathedral steps. In every fist there is clenched a stone. Every face is clenched and blank as stone and the color of Tuscan earth. On the cold still air there seems to rise an odor; it is so recognizable that I scream.

"Pete! Boys! Behind you!"

My scream freezes all movement. The movement on the balcony freezes; the boys freeze, snowballs frozen in their hands; the group below the church steps freezes, clutching its stones.

"They intend to kill us," whispers Mavis.

> *The Lord is my shepherd;*
> *I shall not want.*

Softly chiming the bruised face gazes out, rapturous. Mavis's face is closed. She huddles silently against her doorway.

> *Yea, though I walk through the*
> *Valley of the shadow of death,*

I lift my head, sensing the unseeable bulk of the ancient towers rising above the frozen silence. I feel a grin of terror freeze over my teeth.

Movement down on the piazza: Pete has lowered his arm, slowly turns. He stares at the group of men slowly expanding at the edges as other figures slink from the alleyways to join it. The scarlet H flares like a target across the expanse of white. There is a flare of grins on the faces of the men below as their fists tighten around their stones.

> *I will fear no evil:*
> *For Thou art with me;*

Fury blurs the lens. *Children: they are innocent children.* He hesitates. Then he opens his hand, lets his snowball drop. Slowly he opens his palms. He turns and with palms wide and uplifted he begins to walk across the piazza toward the balcony. His gait is slow, purposeful, steady. At the bottom of the steps he does not pause; ascends them slowly, steadily, one by one. The clot of men separates. Close around him.

> *Thou preparest a table before me*
> *In the presence of mine enemies:*

I wait, grinning. In the piazza the mob waits. The snow falls noiselessly, with a steady intensity, a quickening of purpose.

Movement on the balcony: the black clot parts. The tall figure reemerges. He descends the steps with the same orderly lope. Crosses unhurried to the center of the piazza where Langer and Sascha fall into step at either flank. Steadily they approach the mob at the foot of the church steps. A man steps forward to block them. Pete and the boys stop. A call, *"Li lasciate . . ."* from the balcony. The man steps back, his regard dun, stony.

They ascend the church steps. Pete comes to me, touches my arm. Nods to the girls.

He leads us back down through the empty white alleyways. They follow us. Silently and at a certain exact distance they shadow us to the gates.

As he points the car downhill somebody whispers, *look*. We look back. They are gone. The portals are empty. The blind empty eye is the only break in the walls. The snow comes down steadily, blotting out all trace of the village, obliterating our tracks.

"What did you say to them," Langer murmurs, "what did you say."

"I don't remember. Jesus, I was so scared I couldn't even remember the Italian for 'women and children.'"

— Key, he said.

The heavy gates creaked as he shouldered them open. The old stone palazzo creaked with black and cold.

— You don't need to see me up, I said; I know the way.

— I don't mind, he said. Watch the steps.

We groped our way up the staircase to the landing where the dim bulb forever burns, the plaque forever announces BRUNELLI. I turned there at the door.

— Key? he said.

— I've got it, I said. Thank you.

— My pleasure, he said.

— Goodnight, Pete. Or I guess it's goodbye, I said. Would you like me to drive you to the station?

— No. I've only got one bag. I'll walk.

— Well then take care, Pete. It's been a . . . good semester.

— I love you, he said.

— I know. (My face in the cruel everburning light, cruelly eroded in bonedeep years.)

— Don't cry, he said. It's all right. Please, please, don't cry. I love you.

I turned the key and opened the door. I closed the door and locked it.

6 *winter / spring*

Tinkle, tinkle. The Marchese rings a little silver bell, sets it down again on the quilted silk cardtable cover. "Two no trump," says *maestro* Ferini. "Three hearts," says *dottor'* Mori. "Three no trump," says the Marchese, and to the maid, "*ancora un' po più di whiskey soda, giaccio per la Signora* . . ." "Pass," says Arabella.

Tinkle, tinkle. Ice in glasses; the sough and slap of cards. "*Peh*," explodes Ferini as the last card is swept up, "*bravissima,* Edith. Most courageous, that deep finesse to the knave of hearts." "Not really. Knew it had to be Arabella holding out." "Ah how she does hold out," smiles *dottor'* Mori charmingly. Ferini and the Marchese laugh. Tinkle, tinkle.

losing patience with this. When will you get it through your head that I love you? You keep writing me as if I were just another one of your nice ex-students. Listen: that was not a student back there on those stairs last December. It was a man who knew what he was saying. I don't mess around. When I say I love you that is how it is. That is how it is going to be.

"My dear child here you are at last, just as you promised. Come in, come in, mustn't stand out there in that Arctic blast, such filthy weather, must've been simply exhausting driving down in all this rain. I've a great roaring fire going and the teakettle's steaming away merrily . . . Let me have your coat, you're simply drenched . . . Why my dear mmmm Arabella I b'lieve you're weeping? Come now, come now, must've been a ghastly drive, you look done in, and my dear girl you're terribly thin and pale, winter always seems endless about this time, doesn't it? But of course it's not, all things pass, spring always comes. God renews the world in glory. Revivifies the spirit, yes, marvelous isn't it, God's heartbeat in Nature's pulse, the Resurrection — speaking of which, *tea.* That's the ticket. Come sit here by the fire, dear mmmmm Arabella, and we'll have a great pot of steaming ceremonial tea, and toast, oh simply tons of toast, and this golden honey — the Tuscan clover makes a superb honey, indescribable, and we shall cozen ourselves, have a cozy chat, if of course you can insert a word, and you shall tell me what you've been doing — drat, the kettle's boiled dry. Oh well there's more *water* of course, cistern's brimful, what with all this quality of mercy falling 'round about, haw; haw haw haw haw. Oh dear me, dear *haw* *SPUTTER* me, how marvelous it is, isn't it, how God in His infinite mercy provides so bountifully what one needs?"

Domi has been killed. Out for his afternoon walk with Ugo he broke his leash and dashed across the piazza and was crunched under a car. The old Signori have taken to their beds, Ugo to his room; Agata's face is lumpy as a potato; Lina snuffles as she serves the overdone spaghetti.

"Stupid bloody Ugo." Mavis, redeyed, hoists a strand of spaghetti, lets it slither off, lays down her fork and pushes away her plate. "Imagine, a fullgrown man too stupid to know Domi'd go after a bitch in heat!"

Ugo, last of the Brunelli, terminal shoot of the flowery Renaissance, how did it happen that you came too late to the old knowledge of good and evil? Holed up in your windowless room, walled up stone by stone, icon by icon, into your little monument where history halted centuries ago? Sealed with Naziones *against the draft? Petrified relic in your brownpaper skin and monogrammed codpiece, did you sense that a rush of new air would crumble you to dust? Sad Brunelli: when in your history did you calcify?*

Tinkle, tinkle. On the streetcorners, the little bells of the begging monks. Fat little beggars.

Last summer, walking alone through a little wood in the Boboli, I came upon a young monk and a young woman, sitting on a bench half-hidden under the shrubbery. They sat close together and in silence, their hands folded in their skirted laps. Their faces were locked in a frozen, remote patience.

Now on the winter streets the monks pass in flocks, their habits fluttering in the icy wind, walking with the peculiar motion of men in skirts. The young ones are graceful in their stride but the older ones are ludicrous; almost invariably fat — as if overeating were the remaining sensual pleasure permitted — they thrust out their boots like mechanical clowns, with a droll kicking effect. One of these goose-steppers, sporting floppy galoshes and a transparent plastic slicker over his habit, passed me today. It was the monk I'd seen in last summer's Gardens. How can he be old and fat now, when only two seasons ago he was young, lean, beautiful? What has patience done to him?

Tinkle, tinkle. I drop a few lire into the fat monk's bowl. *Buon appetito.*

seems so useless to be sitting here in a classroom stuffing my mind with these final bits of so-called "learning" when there's so damn much else I could be really learning and really doing. So much to be done in the world outside this ivy tower (yuk yuk) and I'm just sitting here like a little kid getting instructed. It takes all my patience. But I guess I have to have a degree. For one thing, I may decide to start out by teaching — for a while, anyway — back in the ghetto. For another, I figure I've started this, I should see it through. Otherwise the time and money would have been a waste, right? Right now what seems like the biggest waste of all is not being with you. When are you coming back to the U.S.? I wish you'd *write*. Listen: you can't ignore me. Listen: I love you. You can't ignore that. *Write*. I love you.

Listen listen listen. Always the same command. Well, I'm listening, sonny. All night long, slowly roasting on the spit of my dreams, crackle crackle under my pillow, I listen like crazy. Who but a crazy woman would listen to the crackle of a schoolboy's loveletters burning away beneath her pillow?

"That crazy girl. I knew something like this would *SNAP* happen." Eleanor Greene telephones at dawn; only old Agata and I are up, sneaking coffee and a sociable chat together in the kitchen. "Arabella, can you come pick me up? Mort took the car and the kids are all asleep and I need somebody sane."

The Woodcock girl has been brought into the hosiptal. An all-night gas-station attendant up near the Certosa *uscita* found her lying naked and comatose in the ditch by the approach to the autostrada. Mort was the only English-speaking doctor they could rouse. He found her to be suffering from exposure and shock; she has been raped; from her throat to her navel and across her breasts a crucifix has been daubed in her blood. Mort phoned Eleanor to say that the girl will be OK but she is calling for her mother; she needs a countrywoman.

it was me they was after, Mama. I recognized that right off. Mountain men, Mama, just like home, I recognized their faces in spite of that Italian disguise. Even before I saw the stones, hands full of terrible swift stones, I saw from their faces it was that band of Warrior Angels, Mama, comin to claim their vengeance on me

"Stones, my God Morty did they stone her too?"

"No indication, not that kind of bruising or internal bleeding. I'm going to go check with X-ray again, you two stay and just let her talk, she's under sedation and she's semi-delirious, just let her talk."

me they were after but I wasn't scared, Mama, He was with us. They were stoning Him too but He didn't abandon us, Mama, He walked out alone and climbed them stairs right

*into that band of Killer Angels and He bargained His life
for ours. Did you see how He did that, Mama? Walked
alone out over that big piazza all covered with snow*

She lies with her feet dangling over the end of the gurney
and the snowy sheet covering her just to her knees; under
the snowwhite light the sunflower face lies rapturously up-
turned, bleached of all but a white radiance.

"I saw, Billie Jean."

"It's all right now, Billie Jean. Nobody's after you
now. . . . Arabella, do *you* know what she's talking about?
If we could get at —"

"San Gimignano. Last December. Langer was with us,
Eleanor, he must have told you."

"San — Oh yeah, some snowball fight? What's this
about —"

*offered His sweet self as a sacrifice for us. Did you see that,
Mama?*

"I saw, Billie Jean. Lie back down now. It's all right.
You're safe now. Try to go to sleep."

*and then He came back down and laid His sweet hand on
us and He led us to safety down from the mountain. Mama?
You know the hymn? Sing it with me?*

> *He leadeth me,*
> *He leadeth me,*
> *By His own hand*
> *He leadeth me —*

Eleanor Greene looks at me helplessly. I take a deep
breath.

His faithful foll'wer
I would be,
By His own hand
He leadeth me.

"I thought Langer was exaggerating. For heaven's sake, what did *SNAP* happen that day? You're not gonna tell me they really were trying to —"

"I'm not going to tell you anything, Eleanor, because I don't really know."

"You don't *know* whether they —"

"You yourself say that signals between cultures get mixed up, misread. Maybe it just looked that way to us." (And we believed it. Not one of us disbelieved it.) I make motions with the gearshift. ". . . No thanks, Eleanor, I don't think I'll come in for coffee. I have a lot of work to do."

"But you said they *were* throwing stones. Getting hit with a rock, that's a pretty *POP* universal message."

"Maybe they were just having a rock festival." I put the car in gear. "Some kind of festival anyway, who knows. These hill villages, they maintain their, uh, isolated traditions. Maybe they don't want tourists butting in. They must get sick of tourists in San Gimignano. When you come to think of it, Eleanor, these annual floods of tourists must seem sometimes like just another enemy invasion. Even to Florentines. Don't you ever feel, here, like an alien invader?"

"We're used to it," she says amiably.

Going down the palazzo staircase I encounter the old Signora coming up. She is being carried in a sort of fireman's grip between Antonio and Ugo. She is dressed in furs which half-obscure their sweating faces as they lurch up, she swinging perilously on their locked wrists. She is growling with pain but she stops long enough to nod formally as I pass. She rolls up her old eyeballs in an expression which says, Alas, the world is full of suffering for us women.

Lina says the old Signori have been negotiating for over a year with the Barone to get him to put the lift back in operation. "It is perhaps damaged by the flood," she says. "Perhaps? Don't they know?" It is not allowed, Lina explains, to operate a lift without a Certificate of Inspection. The Barone refuses to pay for the inspection, which he considers a suppressive tax upon property owners. *"Ecco. Niente da fare,"* Lina says with a resigned shrug.

can't mean that. You can't mean it when you say you're not coming back to the U.S. You're an American. Not Italian: American. How could you abandon your own country? Listen, we need all the good people we can keep. A lot of kids I know are talking about going to Canada, going to Ireland, going to Sweden. Sure, they're not going to let themselves be drafted. They're not going to let anybody put a gun in their hand and make them go out and kill people. I sure as hell am not going to let them do it to *me*. But I sure as hell am not going to let them drive me out of my own country, either. I'm just arrogant enough to figure I can be of more use here than I could be in Canada. Which is why I'm having this hassle with my draft board over my request for C.O. classification. I don't mind serving, I want to serve — I suppose that sounds disgustingly straight-arrow — but I have to serve in a way I believe in. Listen, you *can't* mean it when you say you're staying over there indefinitely. It is unacceptable. I won't accept it. Listen: I will not accept it. Anyway you have to come back because I have to see you. Jesus I am getting tired of all this. Let's hear no more of that nonsense.

There's something screwy here. The instruments — thermometers, barometers, calendars, clocks — should be checked. A week ago it was quite clearly winter. Everything was frozen solid in icy blocks of stone. History was trapped by the freeze, sealed inside these icecube palaces. Had any of us paid attention we could have walked across the waters of the Arno, frozen in turdbrown wavelets. But I see by to-day's *Nazione* that the ice is breaking up and time coming unstuck, beginning to sluice through in a turdbrown blood-warm gush; for they have murdered Martin Luther King, who was an overpatient man.

"*Eeeeh Dio, Dio,*" groans the Signora, "poor little wife, poor little babies." "I doubt the King woman has little babies," snaps Mavis, "and if she does I'm sure they'll be quite well taken care of. The Americans are keen on pub-licity, y'know, and now they've got a real live Madonna of Sorrows to enshrine." The old Signora clutches her pearls and continues to moan, this time about the old Signore, who has developed a boil on his haunch and cannot move in his bed without the most exquisite pain.

boiled up in me when they killed King. It's been boiling up for a long time everywhere here. If I feel this way — barely able to imagine what it's like — how must they feel? Listen: all this gas I get from you about "impossible." That's boiling up everywhere here and that's what *I*'d call immoral: calling a dream "impossi-ble" before it's been tried. We've all got to *try,* don't we? Don't we?

Seth Greene has been slipped back from Geneva, where he's been guesting it in the villa of an American diplomat, acquaintance of acquaintances. It seems notice has been received that his request for C.O. classification has been rejected, and that he has three weeks to report for his preinduction physical. The Greenes are holding a Council of (anti) War with a hastily gathered group of advisers: an American lawyer connected with a pharmaceuticals-distributing firm in Milan; an American actionist ex-nun; a man attached to the American Friends' Service Committee; and various of the hirsute youths who drift in and out of the Greene scene.

"So whattaya been doing in Geneva, man?" one of these last is saying to Seth. "Oh I dunno," says Seth, smiling gently, "Geneva's, you know, like . . . I'm into poetry, and meditation."

"The way I see it, they won't go for the C.O., they might be delayed some with a higher appeal," says the lawyer. He squints speculatively at Seth. "Or, it just occurred to me, try for 4-F. Any physical disability?"

"Or psychological," muses the nun. "Any Oedipal tendencies?"

"Not with *POP* *me* there aren't."

The AFSC man says, "What's the attitude about noncombat service? I'm speaking here of the 1-AO classification. Could he conscientiously accommodate limited humanitarian duties — medical, say — or does he feel that any participation in the militarist —"

"He doesn't like *war*," Eleanor says, "he's totally non *SNAP* aggressive."

"Homosexuality?" asks the nun hopefully, "bed-wetting?"

"Bee stings? I understand they're extremely hesitant where there's a history of reaction to bee stings," the lawyer says. "Histamine shock —"

"Anaphylactic. Martini?" murmurs Mort.

"Morty. Didn't Seth have asthma once? Remember when he was about two years old, he turned *POP* purple?"

"Asthma!" The lawyer snaps his fingers. "That's it. If there's any evidence that he's prone to asthma attacks, you've practically got it made."

"He turned purple and he couldn't breathe, remember Morty, I thought he'd choked on his *SNAP* cereal but you said it sounded asthmatic — Morty for God's sake stop passing cashews and *remember,* will you?"

"You'll need to get your evidence together. Statements from at least three physicians certifying they've treated him for asthma attacks. That shouldn't give you any trouble, Dr. Greene, finding three colleagues willing to testify to —"

"Shit," says Eleanor suddenly. "This is so shitty."

"You want your son off, Mrs. Greene. I'm assuming you've already worked out the moral goal. I'm merely suggesting the legal means."

"Yeah, you get hung up on method, it replaces the goal," mutters Eleanor wearily. "Morty. Cable Liebman. And let's *POP* see, Velinsky. And maybe we oughtta have a WASP, how about McCallister?"

"Enlist everyone you can," the lawyer advises. "Use anybody who can wield some clout."

"Use? Hey man," murmurs Seth as he drifts past with a bowlful of ice cream, "hey, I'm not into *using* people."

—*È arrivata la posta?*

—*Pazienza, Signora.* It seems it is not yet nine A.M. and the mail does not arrive until nine-fifteen. Insolent Antonio. If he kept the palazzo time correctly there would not be this confusion, this interminable waiting around for little things like mail.

Last night I was leaning on my windowsill gazing down into the cortile, and from it arose the smell of spring. It was unmistakable: the green fragrance of April, wafted up from the dusty old hole. This morning when I opened my eyes the calendar said June.

This time-lag is inexcusable in Florence. It was they, the first modern burghers, who invented our modern time. They saw it for what it really was: a commodity to be bought, sold, and negotiated.

panicky feeling, not having written for so long. But exams are finally finished. I'm now a certified Bachelor of Arts. Another job behind me. This one has seemed so damn long, particularly the last few months. More than anything else the real pain was me here in the U.S. and you there in Italy. It can't go on, this separation. It's *unacceptable,* I told you. Listen: I'm leaving tomorrow morning for Detroit. A real teaching job this time, in a ghetto Junior High. I can't ask you to come there. But I can ask you to come back to the U.S. where at least I can see you once in a while. And then in the Fall maybe I can get a job out in Berkeley . . . Why don't you come help us campaign for Bobby? Listen: he's going to be our next president. He may have bombed in Oregon but he's going to *show* them in California. Can you imagine what it'll be like with a leader like Bobby? You know what he said? "Some people ask 'Why,' I ask 'why not.' " *That* is the Impossible Dream. And Bobby's going to make it possible.

"Charisma's all very well," snorts Mavis, "but you don't really want your country run by a filthy Papist, do you?"

12:30 P.M.

"The guy at the Libreria says Kennedy's been shot." Langer stands over my tearoom table. I smile, unamused, and fold my *Nazione*. "That guy's been holed up in that bookshop a long time," I remark, "which is what happens to archivist types. Did you come in here to clown around or to cadge refreshments? How're your parents? I haven't seen them for a —" "Robert Kennedy." Langer's arms are dangling peculiarly, as if they'd been disconnected at the shoulders. "In the Ambassador Hotel in L.A. about an hour ago." He stands there. He doesn't seem to know what to do with his face, either.

1:10 P.M.

È STATO COLPITO ALLA TESTA, ED IN FIN DI VITA

". . . *gli è stata somministrata l'estreme unzione . . .*" The old Signora rolls her eyeballs to heaven and passes the paper back to me. "Poor little wife," she moans, "all those poor little babies. And another one on the way, eeeeh Dio, the world is full of suffering for us women," and then she announces that the Signore has this very morning had his infected boil removed from his haunch and has eaten some mashed potatoes.

4:00 P.M.

At the jeweler's, picking up some earrings I've ordered for Cassandra's birthday. As he is wrapping them the jeweler says, *"È americana, Signora?"* I nod. He says in English, "You have heard of Kennedy?" I nod; pick up the package. He leans over the counter, a small dapper man with a smooth brown shopkeeper's face. "They are all crazy," he says. "Everywhere. In America and France and China and even here in Italy. Why? Why do things like this happen? What is happening to the world?" I fumble in my purse for lire. "It is the hippies," he says, "it is the youth of today." I put the lire on the counter and turn. "It is the satellites America has placed in space, disturbing the natural balance of the earth," he calls after me, "it is a logical result of your scientists' releasement of the power of the atom."

The Watch, stately, measured, slow. All day I walk the city streets, stopping people now and then at random to ask, Any news? *Lo stesso,* they reply; the same. They look at me slantwise: how does it feel, American? When at last it is evening and I turn wearily in to the cortile Antonio the porter is lounging at the gates, surveying the evening rush, waiting for me. *"Ha sentito da Kennedy?" "Sì." "È capitalisto,"* he says grinning. He follows me as I continue toward the staircase. *"Capitalisto,"* he says again, rubbing his hands together in a workmanly way. And *"Capitalisto,"* he calls after me as I slowly climb the stairs.

8:25 P.M.

The doorbell. In the hall Lina explains I am at table. I excuse myself and go to Langer, standing with his hands hanging at his sides. I lead him into my room. He doesn't look at the chair I offer him. He blinks at me. "We had our

Sophomore party at the Ambassador Hotel last spring," he says, blinking rapidly.

"Langer, he's not dead yet. He's tough, Langer. He's young."

"We're supposed to go home next week." Langer, blinking, raises his clown's eyebrows in a puzzled expression. "I don't wanna go back to L.A. I don't wanna go back to California. I don't wanna go back to the United States."

"He's not dead yet, Langer."

"I don't wanna have to *live* there," he warns.

9:45 P.M.

Sitting in the darkened kitchen at Agata's table, the newsreels flickering against our faces: Bobby giving his triumphant speech; Bobby and the children; Bobby in the ghetto; Bobby and Jack playing touch football on the lawn; Bobby and Rose; Bobby in Africa; Bobby and Ethel; Bobby sweating in the harsh torchy spotlight of politics (. . . *some people ask "why?" I ask "why not?"* . . .); skitter-eyed Ethel standing by, hanging in, fidgeting, grinning. And Bobby — ragged tilted camera with clumsy hands and feet in the way — Bobby pleated on the floor, ragged tilted head cupped in tender black hands, profile stern and astonished, gazing inward; and Ethel, eyes motionless at last. Back to Italy for a studio interview with a famous medical authority. The brain — he cups his hands, decanting it — is like an egg, crated in the skull.

"What's he saying," Langer mumbles standing in the flickering dark with his hands dangling. The great shadow of a head dangles across the screen where the egg, scrambled, is decanting from the crate. "What's he saying."

"*Agata, credi, c'è esperanza?*"

" 'Scuse me, can I . . ." Mavis, creeping in humbly, "don't want to intrude, of course . . ."

"*È giovane, Signora. Corraggio.*" She touches my hand on the table with her old fat one.

"What's she saying," Langer drones.

"He's young, Langer, he's young. There's —"

"Young people don't die, she's saying."

10:50 P.M.

"I'm warning you," Langer drones, "I'm warning you."

Noon

"*Kennedy è morto.*" Antonio, waiting at the bottom of the staircase, makes his announcement. "*Fu capitalisto.*" And so into the historic tense.

Down via Maggio to the piazza newsstand. Sitting on the curb: an American girl; long hair, Boy Scout jacket, jeans, naked feet. She is hunched with her guitar between her knees, staring at a copy of the *Nazione,* peering at it closely as if she were nearsighted. She lifts her head, sees my face, pulls at my skirt. "I just got off the bus," she says. "I been all night on the bus from Grenoble." She waits; to the question in her face I nod. "Dead," she says; "that's what *morto* means?" Again I nod. "Ogod," she says. She puts her cheek against the neck of the guitar. She slides her face down the strings and winds her arms around the guitar's body and rocks it back and forth. "Ogodogodogod," she sobs, rocking. I lay my palm on her hair a moment and then I walk on across the bridge.

Tinkle, tinkle. "Four no trump," says *dottor'* Mori. *"Pass. Ancora un po' più di gin e tonic, giaccio per tutti,"* says the Marchese to the maid. "Pass," says Arabella. *"Scusi?"* says *dottor'* Mori. "She said 'pass,' Gino," says the Marchese. "But —" *dottor'* Mori sputters. "Pass," says *maestro* Ferini very swiftly.

Tinkle, tinkle. Tinkling the ice in her glass Arabella stares out the window onto the terrace, where the late-afternoon sun is hammering away at the little tubbed lemon trees.

"Peh," explodes Mori. "Down three," the Marchese announces, picking up her little gold pen. "That's, mmmm, game and rubber. Arabella and Gino owe, uh, 12,400 lire each."

"The convention," Mori sputters, "the demand convention — do you not remember it, Arabella?"

unacceptable. This country is unacceptable. It has gone mad. We killed him. If this country is us then we are it and we killed him. This country has gone mad with hate, and here in the ghetto it is mad with hate and grief. I feel myself going the same way. I love this country. That is a square thing to say. I get it from all sides when I say it — from white friends my own age, from those blacks who allow me to speak with them as if I could be a friend, or would be if I weren't white. What people don't understand is that a lot of us so-called Young Activists do love this country. But what I feel right now is shame. It is like seeing your mother drunk on the streets.

impossible to think rationally. It's getting worse. You just react,
The way I reacted once and put Carlo in the hospital. And that's
what's dangerous, acting from reaction. I'm leaving the Inner
City. The brothers here say there's too much danger of an inci-
dent, they don't need any more incidents, the whole ghetto could
blow up. It's their necks as well as mine; they can't afford to be
seen with a honkey anymore, and this honkey never was safe on
these streets without one of the brothers as escort. I'm too big
and too white a target. So I split and I wait until it's safe to come
back in. I can't see safety anywhere in this country's madness.
Listen: I've got to see you. I've got to talk to you. If you won't
come back, I've got to come there. That's what I've decided to do.
I've got a job on a construction crew, laying road conduit for the
State. It pays well. Well enough so I ought to be able to buy plane
fare to Italy in a month or so. Listen: write me. I'm coming. I
love you. You might as well make up your mind to accept it.

no answer. Your silence scares me. It is unacceptable, your silence.
You might as well understand I don't accept it. It won't keep me
away.

Dear Mrs. Hatch,

*I think you ought to know that your son is planning a rash
move. If you have any influence over him I urge you to attempt
to dissuade him. He is infatuated with a woman twice his age
who is currently residing in Italy. He is planning to visit her
there. Mrs. Hatch — your son is a very fine upright young man
who should not be allowed to sacrifice himself to irrational and
quite impossible passions. He should settle down with a nice girl
his own age and lead a normal, useful life. There is every indication that he has unusual gifts — perhaps in the field of political
reform, which God knows the country could use; it's not at all
impossible that he might one day be President. An affair with
such a woman — she has a certain notoriety — might very well*

endanger your son's future career. Politics is a tough and some-
times very low-minded business — as you Boston people are cer-
tainly aware — and any stain on your son's personal record might,
if unearthed (as it surely can be predicted, given the nature of
politics and, as I say, this woman's notoriety) bring to an un-
timely end what might otherwise have been a most luminous
career. Again, I urge you to exercise all the power you have as a
mother, to save your son from this terrible error.

— A Friend

know you're still in Florence. I checked with Carlo. I'm arriving
at the Milan airport at 3:35 P.M. Sunday 23rd. I'm hoping — I'm
asking — that you will meet me there. It will save me considerable
hassle and expense, because if you're not there I'll just have to
take the bus to Florence, and if you're not *there* it will take even
more hassle and expense to find you. Which — you better believe
me — I will do. I don't have so much money or time that I can
afford to waste either. But I will spend as much of the first as I
have, and as much of the second as I can, to be with you. I love
you.

7 *summer*

One by one the gates clang open. Baggage rumbles down a long ramp, rotates slowly around the perimeter of a stainless steel servosaucer. There is a Boy Scout Knapsack which has been circling 1,826 times. Over the loudspeakers boardings are announced for Roma, Cairo, Parigi, Cannes. Flights arrive at Milano every 13.4 minutes. The one from Boston eventuated 28 minutes ago and the last of its 102 passengers have streamed through the turnstiles and been greeted with screams by lovers and families; babies have been thrust at sobbing papas and grandmothers united with sisters-in-law and smugglers have slipped their packets into each others' décolletages. The next flights are from Copenhagen and Istanbul. I move down the line of plate-glass information booths. *Signore, per piacere — l'ultima fuga da Boston — ? Arrivò lontano fa, Signorina.* That long ago; already history? I move from booth to booth hoping to improve the odds. At the very last one I am informed that the next flight from America may perhaps arrive New Year's Eve 1976,

barring another Revolution. I turn to rework my way back-
ward down the line — one must negotiate with these Italians
— and I bump into a wall. Two great gates slowly swing
open to receive me.

— You're thinner.
— It's been a thin time. He looks down at his hands on
the trattoria tablecloth. They are tanned very deep brown.
He opens and closes them into fists. There are shadows in
the tan sockets under his cheekbones. The blond hair by
contrast looks as if it had turned white overnight.
— You're so brown. I've never seen you tanned.
— Outside work. I've never seen you in a summer dress.
He is still looking at his hands, opening and closing them.
You look beautiful in a summer dress, he says.
— Thank you, I say.
— My pleasure, he says.
The waiter appears. *Ora una dolce? Formaggio?*
His eyes flatten. Blue and flat as the summer sky. Then
they deepen again. *Niente, grazie,* he says. *Allora il conto,
per favore.*
— I'll get it, I say when the waiter brings the check.
— Thank you, he says.
— My pleasure, I say.

"Are you tired?"
"I'm never tired."
Never have I seen a man look so tired. "Tell you what,
Pete, let's go over to the Galleria and have a coffee and then
we can go to the hotel, it's just around the corner from

there, you can check in, there's a room reserved for you, you can rest a bit before dinner —"

"A room," he says with care, "for me."

"It hasn't got a bath, I hope you don't mind, I thought with your limited funds you'd want something less —"

He touches my arm. "Hey. It's OK. Anything's OK." Takes a deep breath, lets it out gently, as if his ribs were glass. "I'm here. At this particular moment anything and everything's OK. Just . . . take my word for that."

I will take his word for that. You have to begin somewhere.

"Your son. You told them I was your *son*."

He stands over me as I sit on the edge of the hotel chair, my hands fists in my lap. I'm not used to beginnings. "I'm not used to this," I whisper.

"You think *I* am?" Suddenly he breaks his stance, lurches over to the bed, heaves himself down, lets out a mighty — my God — laugh. "Your son! You figured they'd believe you?" Flails around in helpless glee. "They'd actually believe you've got a son my age?"

Do you figure, sonny, it's a question of belief? Other people can see my face. Can it be that you can't?

"Well then, I guess I'll let you —" I rise. He has snapped open his suitcase, lifted out his toilet-kit.

"Can I use your bathroom?"

"Certainly. My room's — bathroom's just down the hall."

"You shoulda got adjoining. I don't like the idea of sneaking down hotel corridors."

"Sneaking? I . . . Nobody's going to be sneaking —"

"Listen." He comes to stand over me. "Listen to me. You're a very wise woman. You may be the wisest person I know." His eyes are sockets of intensest blue. Under the tan his face is pale, kiln-glazed. "But you don't *want* to be wise about this. You don't even want to believe it. You're scared." He takes a deep, measured breath. "Listen, I'm scared too. You think I'm not scared? Oh baby I am so scared. But I trust it. I trust the way I feel, even the fear. Fear's part of anything huge. I had it in the ghetto all the time. I had it before every football game when I was a kid. I trust it. I got to."

He lays his two hands on my head. Lightly, barely the touch of them, two great palms formally and with great tenderness and great fear laid over my head. I close my eyes.

"Trust it. Trust me," he pleads. "I'll take the responsibility. It sure is my responsibility, isn't it?" His voice cracks. Inside it is so young, it is like the crack in a little baby's skull between the two hemispheres of bone which have not yet knit firmly together. I can see down the crack to the assailable newness inside. He coughs and the bone knits firm again. "The name of the game," he says sternly, "is trust. OK?"

I sit here folded in my little packet of skin which is much smaller than I remember. Naked and unsheltered my body feels like a bird's, the bones inside light and strutted; they keep wanting to separate from their sockets and flutter around. I hold my elbows tight in against my ribcage tightening the little filaments that wind me around holding everything together in the packet.

He ought to see that I can't let go to loosen the little threads, he will somehow have to do that himself. I can't instruct him. It is his beginning: every man must reinvent his own beginnings. Even if I could remember how it used to be managed I'd never instruct him because then it would be like being unwrapped by ghosts. Fumbling at knots so tiny and numerous no more than half of them were ever located. I am wrapped in a cat's cradle of invisible filaments knotted so intricately that the grain of a whorl on a fingertip sliding the wrong way along a strand could snag and rip it. If they were to look at me in certain lights they would see an aureole around my naked body which is the frayed ends of strands torn rather than untied. Every woman looks like that in certain lights . . .

His packet is not hollow but solid clear through, most densely and economically packed, secured with straps of muscle . . .

Why doesn't he begin? Reach out a finger and run it across at least one surface thread? Maybe he's afraid his hand is too large or the patterns of his fingerprints too coarse and young and unworn. Older men have fingertips like burglars', sanded with practice to an exquisite smoothness which, even when it catches, can barely be felt.

Trussed immobile in his straps of muscle he watches me helplessly. I feel his gaze between my shoulderblades as I sit on the edge of the bed pressing my palms prayerfully between my trembling thighs, waiting for him to take the responsibility.

I turn on my hip. I present my face which is so assailable and I whisper, "I'm scared."

His eyes again become sockets of intensest blue. "I am too." And having stripped himself down to this final nakedness he reaches out desperately to the illusion of mine.

— I can't understand it. Oh God I cannot understand it.
I can. Bone-fear which before was a live and clacking thing has turned old, cold, still.
— It's all right, Pete, it's perfectly natural. It's all right . . . My hand and my murmuring wash over him. You've come so far, I murmur, it's been such a long trip, think of the miles in one day, it is perfectly natural . . .
Until at least belief overcomes him, his panic is exhausted; he abandons the need to understand and sleeps the arduous sleep of trust.
And I gather up my bag of bones and lug them down the corridor to my own room where I lay them down and pick them over, one by one, marveling at their weight and trying to imagine their unimaginable antiquity.

Out of the morning's young power the world recreates itself a young era. On the windowsill a tray of sunlight and fragrant bread and sweet butter and jam and black coffee and napkins crisp as nannies' skirts.

He comes slickhaired and dripping from my shower, ravenous: "Coffee," he commands; and "what are you, writing this early in the morning?"
I lay the journal aside. Sitting in my gray silk caftan I pour him coffee. He receives the cup from my hand. Slow awakening courses like light over his face. The moatblue eyes deepen, clearing.

"You are so beautiful," he exults (the sun is at my back). "Beautiful," and he leans to kiss my hair. "Like one of those, uh, Spanish shawls. I didn't know it was so long. Why do you put it up? Don't put it up anymore," he commands, "leave it long."

He is sweetsmelling as a freshbathed baby's bottom. His and the morning's light flood my room. I duck my face from it, shyly, under my Spanish shawl of hair. He eats, and crumbs cling sweetly to his lips. He washes them away with the last of the coffee.

Sitting under the great glass dome of the Galleria, sunshine streaming in, we anchor the map with our *cappucino* cups. "Here" — my finger traces from Milan east — "to here is about a day's drive." We will take back roads over to the Adriatic Coast, find a little village where we can swim and stay a night or two before we head over toward Arezzo.

"When are we supposed to be at this place?"

"Tim's expecting us on the twenty-eighth. He's leaving the next morning for his London holiday. We'll have —"

"Does he have to be there? Couldn't he put the key under the mat or something?" (He frowns. Oh God he frowns!)

"Do you mind, Pete? He wanted to tell me about some things, explain about the pump and the water and something about the refrigerator, it's all so tricky and a bit primitive — But if you mind his being there when we arrive I suppose I could —"

"Why should I mind his being there? It's his house. I meant if we're delayed, found someplace we wanted to stay an extra day or something, we wouldn't be pushing to meet some schedule. I don't want schedules." He picks up my finger and moves it gently off the map. "Or maps." Folds it neatly. "We don't need schedules and we don't need maps. OK?"

Slumberous with noon wine I lie back in our pocket of roadside grasses and under the crook of my arm observe how particles of sunlight cluster around his head and flake off his chin as he munches his bread. I doze.

Open my eyes directly into intensest blue. He is leaning on one elbow gazing down into my naked face, from which sleep has stripped back the flesh-covers. Before I can snatch them up again he bends and touches his mouth to mine. His kiss is curved, tentative.

Now! While there's nothing between us!

But he raises his head and rolls away and I hastily smooth back the covers and we sit up, blinking in the sun. "I s'pose we better hit the road again," he says.

His breath smelled like wine and apples and warm grasses.

Heat: the car rides rolling waves of it, bucking the low dips and swells of the long straight Po valley, floating in the yellowish summer-heat haze.

"Hey."

"Mm?"

"This place we're staying — this farmhouse. The guy who owns it, you say he's a friend of yours?"

"Tim? Very old friend. Very dear friend."

"How old? How" — he clears his throat but too late to cover the crack — "dear?"

"Oh old enough. And very dear." The car gives a lurch between the last two words. "As dear as only a guy in his eighties can be."

"Eighties . . . I s'pose he's as fond of you as you are of him?"

"Tim's fond of everybody."

"And particularly of you?"

"You sound jealous."

"Jealous? Me?"

"Then why the grim look? An old guy in his eighties. Ridiculous."

"Ridiculous? Listen, maybe you don't know all that much about men. My great-grandfather was eighty years old when he married —"

"Well yes, old people often marry for companion —"

"— and he had three children, the last when he was eighty-seven. Now do you still say it's ridiculous?"

". . . I say" — weakly — "that you New England men must be something else."

Later: "And furthermore. I. Am. Never. Jealous."

He reaches over to tap my knee with one severe fore-finger. Then lolls back behind the wheel, full of himself.

A village, pink in the rosy evening. I wait in the car, parked in the dusty little piazza, dead-center of community interest. Leaning against the *macelleria* doorway curtained with strings of plastic beads the shopkeeper lips a toothpick and stares. On the church steps a clump of *ragazzi* stops bouncing its soccer ball and stares. The men at the table outside the *tabaccheria* pause in their card game and stare. A dog comes up and sniffs the tires. A bigbosomed young matron in clogs pushes a stroller across the cobbles, she and her baby bouncing jauntily; she stops and stares. The dog pees on one tire and goes on to sniff the next. The Peugeot seems to swell, filling the piazza.

Pete busts out of the doorway of the little *albergo*. All eyes track as he lopes across the piazza, sticks his head in the car window.

"OK. We got a room. Not very big but it looks clean. Bath's down the hall, washbasin in the room. And get this. Seven hundred and fifty lire apiece *including*" — he raps my shoulder triumphantly with the backs of his knuckles — "dinner and breakfast. How about that? A room and two meals for a buck-twenty apiece!"

"*A* room? But we . . . but I . . ." Shut up. I will probably never get to see a New Englander any happier.

The little old innkeeper serves us our supper of ravioli and red wine and retires behind the bar where he twiddles the knobs of an old radio and watches us. His little old wife comes to stand in the kitchen doorway with her hands folded under her apron and watches us. Two old men, three teenage bucks, and a dog slope in and nursing two vermouths, a split Coke, and fleas, they watch us. Pete schlupps wine and belts ravioli.

Presently I lay down my fork. "Pete. They keep watching us."

"Why not? We're the only action in town." Throws back his head to drain his glass. "Also," he announces, banging his glass down contentedly, "they probably never saw a woman as gorgeous as you. Let's have another demi of wine. What the hell, it's only a hundred and twenty lire."

"Pete? What did you tell them when you registered?"

"Tell them? Oh. I told them you were my mother."

"My God. No wonder. One room. One bed —"

"Isn't that what you told 'em in Milano? Isn't that the act?" He is grinning. "Simmer down, beautiful. I didn't tell 'em anything. I just handed the old guy the passports. The name of the game," reaching out to tap my hand with his forefinger, "is anonymous. You got that?"

The Italians will have another name for it, sonny; not so sweet in any language.

"Signore? Un po' più di vino — bianco, per favore."

"White wine?" I don't need any more wine. Hasn't he noticed I shouldn't have much wine? *"White* wine, Pete? I thought you liked red better."

"Never mind. Drink it."

I drink it. The name of the game, I guess.

"Is it —?"

"Yes. Yes . . . Push."

". . ."

"It's fine. You're fine. Now . . . Just . . ."

". . . ! It's not. Oh *god.*"

"It's all right. It's all *right,* darling. Pete, shhhh now, it's

perfectly natural, it's still strange, a strange place, it's been
a long day and a long hot drive and you're tired —"

"I. Am. Not. Tired."

"— and you've had quite a bit of wine —"

"I have? Could that affect —"

"Of course it can, darling, didn't you know that? Didn't
you know that alcohol, sometimes even a very small amount
of it and particularly in situations that are mmmmm delicate and new —"

"It is not all that new."

". . . well. But new, you know, with . . ." An old. Old
Old old. Old old old old oldoldold

"— somebody I really love. Is that it? I can't make love
to the only woman I ever loved. Jesus H. *Christ.*"

— Hey. Listen. Could it have been the wine?

— Of course. It could have been the wine, it could have
been any number of perfectly natural

— I'll kill that guy when I get back. I'll kill him.

— Good heavens. Who?

— That so-called buddy of mine on the construction crew
who told me white wine's an aphrodisiac.

— Hey. Over there on that hill. A medieval fortress.

— And a village. It looks so ancient, Pete. I can't even
find it on the map. I wonder what its name

— Put that map away. We don't need maps. Didn't I say
we don't need maps? We don't need names for anything?

Nor does he need to rescue anybody today.

Hill country. The road uncoils in spirals of blinding heat. He blinks sweat from his eyes as he hauls the wheel of the Peugeot around the tight curves. The sky burns white with heat. The cypress spiking the horizon are bleached with heat. The poppies at the roadside lie crushed palely under the sun; meadows of barley droop limp and still. Stopping to picnic there is no sound, not even the hum of locusts, under the roar of the Tuscan sun. Standing beside the car, peach juice and sweat dripping richly from his chin, he suddenly grins. "Man." *"Cosa?"* "I was just thinking" — he leans forward and lets the pit drop from his mouth — "about three hours from now." "What's in three hours?" "That's when I figure we hit the coast and you climb into that black bikini I saw in your suitcase. Man." "How little it takes sometimes," I say faintly, "to make a growing boy happy." "Yeaaaaaah."

Waist-deep in the tepid water I watch him stroke powerfully away from me until his head is no bigger than a blond otter's. Behind me on the beach a group of children paddle squalling around the pilings, while their mamas call to them from the sand. *Mari-i-ia, Gi-i-no, fai cau-u-uto!* Be careful, children . . .

I duck under, swim a few strokes, tire, turn on my back and float. Coming upright presently I push the hair from my face and squint out over the colorless expanse of the Adriatic. A sea even more archaic, historic —

Where is he?

Anto-o-o-nio, vie-e-e-eni, è ta-a-a-ardi . . . Late. What time is it? Where is he? Oh it is late, late! Behind me the sun has set, the children have vanished, the mamas have packed them up and taken them home, the beach and the sea and the sky are empty

SNORT His head pops up ten yards away, grinning, pleased with its trick. The sun comes out and the mamas return to the beach and the children begin to play in the water and softly they call to each other *Fai cau-u-uto* . . .

— But I still don't get what made you so mad.

— I explained, Pete, I wasn't mad, I was just . . . thinking.

— Yeah, well, don't think like that again. You scared hell outta me. Man, I never saw a look like that on your face. Just don't you think like that anymore, OK?

The smell of his skin is of sun, and wild grasses, and salt. The juices of his heat and youth and struggle.

How heavy he is. I'm pinned beneath a redwood log. Even he is immobilized by his own weight. I brace my elbows. I cup the heels of my hands against the hard rack of bones below his belly. I heave. Pushing, sweating, half-drowned in sweat, we begin the nightly lesson. *Let us discover the question.* We struggle, trying to break through to the question.

— You notice how crowded that town was? Loaded with Frenchmen, Germans, tourists overrunning the place. What're all these people doing in an Italian beach town?

— It's cheap. They're vacationing, like us.

— Yeah, well, I wish they'd take their cheap vacations

someplace else and leave Italy to — what're you laughing at?

— *Te. Italiano, ti amo. Riso perchè ti amo* . . . What was that kiss for?

— The *ti amo*. You finally got around to telling me you loved me. Now maybe someday you'll get the guts to tell me in English.

— How far now?

— I'm not sure. I think only a few kilometers.

Inside the car time has kinked up tightly, winds around me like an induction coil. Around every curve a current of ancient vistas. The Val d'Arno quivering in afternoon haze; bluegreen sheen on grapeleaves; olives ripples of silver. A brook plunging from a grassy hillside down under an old stone bridge, a sudden eddy of coolness; the mnemonic smell of water and moss floods my brain like a gas. Hot tires squall around the bend and suddenly a screech of the brakes: in the middle of the road, two white oxen drawing a cart in which stands a ruddyfaced peasant. As we swerve past, his cry — *buoi, buoi!* — floats back.

His name is Aurelio.

The countryside is like the second after an explosion, quivering violently at its fullest moment of fragmentation, blooming against the scrim of memory.

— Hey. You OK? You look sort of pale.

— I'm OK. It's just been . . . so long since I was here.

— I thought you said you visited last winter?

— So long since I've been here in the summer.

Twenty years, since that summer.

"My dear girl. At last! I shall be right down. Let me get on a shirt." Tim withdraws from the high window, appears a moment later up on the porch; descends the steps, arms wide and welcoming, long old-man's legs bandying carefully below the tattered shorts. "My dear Arabella, how brown you look! Such a change from the wan maiden I saw at Christmastide. And this — Ah, Peter! Welcome my dear boy. I'm delighted, simply delighted, to meet you at last. Your mother's been so looking forward to your arrival and now here you are, aren't you?

"Good heavens, Arabella, you wrote me he was a big fellow but you didn't say he was a veritable young Goliath! My word, he'd make two or three of you, wouldn't he? . . . You must be simply wrung out from the drive. Hideously hot. Beastly. Come along inside at once where it's cool and have some tea. Dear boy, leave the cases, you can lug everything up later, oodles of time, they're quite safe here in the courtyard, y'know, unlike Florence . . . Ignore the confusion. I've been sorting through some things and of course packing and so forth. Trying to get this samovar in m'valise. Thought it'd make a rather posh wedding present for m'nevvew, don't you think mmmmmm Arabella? Quite a decent piece really, picked it up in a Cairo bazaar in '23 I think it was, snatched it out from under Lady Mary Haversham's nose — s'mattrofact it was '24, that was the year she and Percy were out collecting bird specimens of the Upper Nile for the Geographic Society.

"P'raps you'd rather have coffee, mmmmmm Peter? You American lads — tea? Splendid. S'pect there's no coffee anyway. However there're *eggs*, Arabella, Peppina just brought another two dozen this morning, can't have too many eggs, can one? She'll bring 'em several times a week if you want, simply arrange it with her. If you need things like butter or milk she'll fetch 'em for you in the village, pedals in on her bike a couple times a week — I prefer to walk m'self, it's only nine kilometers to Loro, delightful walk, one never tires of it — obliging little wench, Peppina, you may remember her grandparents, people still live up the road, all eight — no, ten with the latest babies — their fields are over there to the north. And of course the closest neighbors are the Berninis — you *do* remember the dear Berninis, Arabella? Aurelio and Gina? You'll see them of course, Gina comes in to do for me a bit, imagine you'll want to keep her on to make the beds and do up the pots and take the washing — and Aurelio still tends the garden, oh most strictly, terrible tartar really about picking the vegs. Dressed me out, Aurelio did, for planting all those daffodil bulbs in his veg-plot, I had to sneak out and do it in the evening, and then of course when they came *up* *HAW* *twittle* kept bringing 'em in pretending they were onions *HAW* SPZZZ! Oh dear me dear me such a dear man, Aurelio. Smatterofact he planted the entire garden this year, I had an attack of rheumatiz, such a beastly wet spring, creaked around like an old gate. And that dear man put in the whole perennial bed, real gesture of devotion y'know, some people consider flowers a scandalous waste of good soil. Splendid people, Berninis, dear old friends . . .

"Do have some more toast, Peter. Can't let you shrivel

away to a shadow, can we? My word, Arabella, however did you manage to produce such an enormous son?"

"Here I am rattling on and you two probably perishing for a washup and a nap. I imagine you'll want the front bedroom, Arabella, it has a simply delightful view of the orchard and of course the valley. And Peter across the way, it's smaller but there's a desk in there, I understand you're a studious lad. Splendid. So few young people take time out to ponder things nowadays. Always in a rush, as if there weren't time to do it all. Plenty of time for the young, of course. I can see you're a thoughtful lad, a listener. Not much else you can do, can you, with me babbling on like an old brook? Thoughtful, yes, like your mother at that age — why, you must've been almost exactly Peter's age when I first knew you, Arabella. My word, amazing, twenty years."

Where d'you want this bag? Mother.
Pete. Please
Hey. Hey, are you crying? Aaaah don't. Come on, please don't. I was just kidding. Listen, I don't really care if you told him you were my — Jesus. Don't. Ah baby, baby, don't . . . Here. Wipe your face . . . C'mon, that's better. Listen: there's only now, right? No past, no anything, nobody but us. There's only now, OK?

"Let's see now. What splendors can we scrape for supper?" Tim rubs his palms together and looks brightly around the kitchen. Lifts the lid of an enormous iron pot standing in a windowsill. Peers in, ruminates, replaces the lid. "Must chuck that out eventually," he mutters. Looks into a few more, humming speculatively, lids them. "There might be some cheese," he says hopefully. "Definitely eggs. Can't have too many eggs on hand, y'know."

I announce it will be my pleasure to take us out for dinner. But first — producing the gift bottle of gin — we shall have genuine American-made martinis.

Driving to the tiny village of Loro Ciuffenna, five miles up the road. Cerulean evening, smell of fields and water and heat. Empty of luggage the Peugeot rattles like a truck. Tim sways in the front seat, broadbrimmed poet's hat nudged rakishly askew, long gray hair fluttering lankly in the blowing window.

"Up that hill — see the lane there — there's the little church I go for early Sunday morning mass — you may remember it, Arabella, I b'lieve you went with me once? — quite old, y'know, fourteenth century, terribly run-down now, very poor parish of course, they've built a grander new *chiesa* outside Loro. Only ones of us who hang on, me and a half-dozen old girls, they send the parish priest round once a month. Send round the monthly sermon too, same pastoral message all over, y'know. Last month it was simply glorious, m'dear, we were treated to a sermon on the evils of the Pill. There we sat, th'seven of us, and not a uterus amongst us, HAW HAW *SPTZZZ*! Omy Omy, life is so marvelously rich, isn't it?

"My dear mmmmm Arabella how splendid of you, such

a treat, driving out to dinner in style, hope you'll enjoy this little restaurant. Modest, of course, only three or four tables, village's a bit far off the autostrada for tourists. Let's hope Gino's caught some trout today. He poaches it divinely with a bay leaf and some scallions. If there's no trout there's a pepperoni sort of thing with eggplant . . . And here we are already, such a dashing driver you are, my dear Peter, *whups* gone past it dear boy, first place in the village, should've warned you. Too narrow to crank this enormous thing round, best you just push on through town, there's a little piazza just over the bridge by the old mill you can turn . . . Quite a deep gorge as you can see, old waterwheel there in medieval times but now the grindstone's run by electricity of course . . . That veg stall over there, has excellent melons but the one over by the *tabaccheria* isn't so dear, can't imagine why. By the by there's a very good butcher shop up that little street there, go in and tell Paolo that the Professore sent you. There's another butcher over by the Postal Telegraph — one-eyed fellow, has good meat but a frightful head for figgers, tends to overcharge. Stung me once on some tripe, the wretch . . . Well and here we are, *whups,* overshot again dear boy. However. Road's clear, just back up into this farmyard — *mind the geese* — and pull 'er round, splendid. Americans are such dashing drivers."

"My dear Gino you've quite outdone yourself. No no no, couldn't cram in another bite, Arabella. Not the trencherman I once was, alackaday. Have to surrender the baton to the young hearties like this one here. Ah Peter m'bucko, the delights of the flesh, eh? Here. Finish off the cheese, lad."

No, Pete. *No.* Not with Tim upstairs.

Jesus. He can't hear us. He's a mile away and the walls must be three feet thick.

It's not that. It's a . . . courtesy.

Let me ask you something. Why do you want to deceive him about us? He's old, he's wise, he must've seen everything. And after all, he's — well, he's a bit eccentric himself. If I interpreted what he was saying about the old days, and the sacraments of the flesh.

Homosexuality was considered quite respectable, at least among the late Victorian bohemians and poets, like Greek tradition . . . And for a man like Tim it *was* transcendent and sacramental. It's not that, Pete. It's a question of . . . courtesy. Eccentricity's one thing, propriety's another.

You think he wouldn't consider our uh — you know — transcendent and sacramental? You know what *I* think? I think he knows about us.

If he does, do we have to force it on him? Your generation puts such value on brute honesty. Some of us still choose to ignore brute honesty in favor of the amenities.

So what're the amenities here? I don't quite

The amenities here consist in the opportunity to choose between ignoring a fact and having your face rubbed in it . . . Pete, I don't care if he can hear us or not, I just don't want

OK. The name of the game is amenities. But just for tonight . . . Jesus. The waste of a whole goddam night. The *waste.*

"My dear I wouldn't hear of it. Aurelio's boy is running me into Arezzo for the early bus to Florence. Taxi to the train and then in Rome me old chum Perry will scoop me up and chuck me onto the London plane.

"Splendid morning. Going to be hot again. You might have to irrigate the peas today, m'dear. Mind you don't spray, causes mold. But you know that of course, you once told me your mother's a gardener. How is your mother, m'dear? Oh, I am sorry. One is so stranded sometimes, just surviving . . . What time d'you have?

"Oh not yet six, plenty of time for a dash more tea. I'm excited as a child. Let's see, what've I forgotten? Had a list somewhere, mind's like a colander, have to make lists. Drat . . . Well the two of you should manage swimmingly. Can't imagine anything that young giant of yours couldn't handle. Just tell him to mind the wick in the fridge. When he re- fills it — that tin of kerosene under the kitchen stairs there — make sure he removes the glass carefully. Frightful nui- sance if the glass breaks. Finally found a shop in Arezzo that'll blow me another but fearfully expensive — here, I'll scribble the address . . .

"The *water*. You must keep checking the cistern — it's in the cellar m'dear, I showed it to Peter last evening, told him to make sure it's at the proper level. Otherwise the pump will need to be —

"Oh mercy there's Aurelio's boy. Do I have m'tickets? And your check of course, your blessed rent check which made it all possible — You have my London address? Splen- did. Well, m'dear, take care. Have yourselves a lovely holiday. I know you will, I can see it in your faces, a sacramental grace there, such a splendid reunion for you —

"No no no, don't wake Peter. Let the lad sleep. The young need it, consume it like gas. Whereas we can't afford much of it I fear — *Vengo, vengo subito, Mario!* Goodbye, m'dear, goodbye. Enjoy yourselves. God bless you both. Such a fine young lad. Do watch the water in the cistern."

8 summer

Down in the meadow, wet with grasses. The wet grass
grows all around all around. Crouched in the crotch of the
old apple tree, jeans soaked to the knees. Spitting out a
worm. That's what the early bird gets.

Buoi! Aarrgh! Buoi! Awakened at dawn to the cries of
Peppina's uncle urging his oxen down the lane. The creak
of the cart fades down the hill beyond the orchard. I lie
breathing the newness of the morning. I am alone in my
narrow bed. During the night I arose from his side, I came
to my room and to the coolness and calm of my own sheets.
The energy of that big body, powerful even in sleep, rum-
bled along my flank and thrummed at the edge of my con-
sciousness so that I couldn't sink into the solitude of dreams.
He groaned and gnashed his teeth as I slipped away. Even
in his sleep he keeps struggling to break through to me.
Doggedly pursuing knowledge in its Biblical sense. How
mightily he labors at his lessons. *Teach me,* he pleads with

his body. But perversely, against my own will, I cannot instruct beyond the first simple lesson.

I pick up apples wet from the grass and pile them into my basket. Amble back up the rutted lane with the thistles brushing my hips; past the orchard and olive grove and vegetable garden and the flowers, all heavy with morning. The sky sheds a whitish radiance that presages another scorching day.

I dump out the apples on the kitchen table and begin to peel and core them. They are the toughest little green apples God ever made. I can barely get the knife through them and the white flesh turns brown instantly. I cut myself and my brown flesh turns red. A bride I am and virgin cook, as well. This show of ritual blood exalts me. Apple after apple I pare and core and dice until the basket is empty and then I boil them and I grate some nutmeg into them and when they've begun to surrender I put in a huge pat of butter and sugar and a little — what? — flour and scrabbling around find — what else? — a lemon and I put that in too with *ooops* a few seeds. And when he comes sleepy to the kitchen the air is marvelous with apples and coffee, which I serve him along with bread and honey and an omelet I've forgotten to salt. He eats, and his face slowly floods with awakening; and his face is new as Adam's and so beautiful that I, sitting across the table smoking my first cigarette and watching shyly, get up and wander to the front door. I stand with my hands in my hip pockets, looking out over the fields, which awakening have begun to sing as if it were the first morning of Creation.

Our closest neighbors are the Rossis, the tribe of *banditti* who live five hundred yards up the lane in their sprawling ramshackle compound. At two o'clock when Pete and I trudge past on our daily hike they are all lolling around the water trough in the courtyard or hanging out the windows of their main quarters above the stables. They stop dead in their whittling or arguing or chicken plucking — it is the siesta hour — and watch us pass. We offer the prescribed *buona sera* and at this they break, as a man, into broad grins of varying colorations and gaps; chorus back their *buona seras* in varying cackles and growls, and grin after us until we're out of sight around the vineyard. When eleven-year-old Peppina brings us our eggs and bread she stands in the door wearing the same grin, which looks as if it holds in barely containable hysteric mirth. We invite her inside; she claps both her hands over her face in an explosion of giggles, and sits at the kitchen table with us drinking her Coke as if at any moment she were going to die, simply die, of glee. Either this is a family tic, or something about us is just too much.

Back from our constitutional — eight kilometers uphill, my God, to a dusty village of a half-dozen houses, and twelve kilometers back down via "shortcut" through brushy gullies — I am almost overcome. Cannot admit exhaustion but can blame heat, some ninety degrees of it. "Sweat's good for you," says Pete. "We gotta keep you in shape . . . condition, I mean," he adds, eying me.

"What for?" Smartass reflex I immediately regret. His

reflex is a leer; then over his face flashes astonishment and then speculation. Eyes narrow, speculating.

"Well," I say faintly, "I guess I'll go bathe, take a little—"

"Nap. Yeah. Time for a nap." He ambles speculatively toward me. I back up. Pass my hand feebly over my hair. "Nap, yes, I'm really awfully tired, it's so hot . . ." I am *tired*. I am hot. I am much too tired and hot for a

"Nap," he says, swooping and scooping.

Carried to the bedroom I am too tired and hot, oh *dio*, even to make a fuss.

. . . *Aaaaaaahhhhhh* . . .

A groan like a sigh and in little more time than this it is at last accomplished.

Come morning: he rises like a god. Petals and feathers clinging to his breast. Hurls thunderbolts from the shower. Fills the kitchen doorway with the Presence. Stands with towel-draped loins, commanding obeisances. Humbly his handmaiden approaches bearing laurels to crown him and trays of sweetmeats for his delight and with a trumpetry of joyful noises unto his Lordship bears him off on a flowered litter, nymphets frolicking fore and aft, and *whups* crowns him again.

"How about that," he says reverentially. "In the morning, too . . ." And presently, "Hey. C'mere."

Sitting at the caretaker's long wooden table belting back grappa. Cool in here—enormous limestone cave of a dwelling—while outside the four o'clock sun hammers away at the fields. We've come in a ceremonial capacity to present our credentials and petition for a modest treaty. Peppina is our go-between, has handled the niceties of arrangements and introductions. She is now giggling at the far end of the table with the caretaker's daughter who is her school chum.

When we arrived the caretaker — Salvatori is his name — was napping, but his wife sent the girl to awaken him. The wife is a spare farmwoman with a shy dark reamed face. Wordlessly she gestures us in and then seems not to know what to do with us. We stand in the dim bareness of the farmhouse awaiting the caretaker's appearance. He comes in briskly — small, wiry, surprisingly light-eyed — shakes our hands, ushers us into the main room and seats us ceremoniously at the table, so central to the peasants' domestic life it might as well be the marital bed; the room is bare of everything but a sink and a great fireplace. The caretaker brings grappa and three glasses. The wife sits slightly apart from us. She looks years older than her husband; now that she is at her own table she has a watchful, dignified calm.

We raise our glasses. Pete and I sip cautiously — *wow* — and the caretaker downs his in one quick thrust, pours himself another, plants his elbows, and opens communications. Salvatori is a man, plainly, of serious thoughts. We discuss the weather, the crops, the coming harvest. The late rains have caused some difficulties though there are benefits, too. The feed is bountiful for the birds. This part of Tuscany, he explains, is a pheasant and dove preserve. He is in charge of this district; he raises pheasants and turns the young loose in the fields at hunting season. He is also the caretaker for the estate of the Conte — doubtless we have noticed the large villa up on the hill above Loro? — who owns much of the land around here. The Conte and his son and guests are in occupancy during the hunting season . . . He pauses.

This is the opening for negotiations — Peppina has hinted loosely at the nature of our petition — but Pete either does not perceive this or chooses to wait. I hesitate. Decide my inauguration of action would be improper. The caretaker, who has been watching, flicks me a glance of approval and refills our glasses.

"You are enjoying your stay here, Signora?" He addresses himself directly to me for the first time. I say I think the Tuscan countryside is the most beautiful in the world. He is pleased; when I add that I am from fabled California, he considers it a personal compliment. *"Ecco. Bravissima, Signora,"* he murmurs.

He turns to Pete. "The Signora is your sister?" he says urbanely.

"Mamma," calls Peppina from the end of the table; *"è la sua Mamma,"* and has to use both hands to stuff back her giggles.

"Accidente." The caretaker, with the mild swearword of astonishment, returns the compliment deftly doubled: high-toned foreign women are not usually let in on domestic cameraderie. "Surely the Signora is far too young?" I smile, a bit flirtatiously as is required, and indicating the grappa tell him that I'm feeling younger every minute. He refills my glass over my protests. We exchange complimentary grins, a quick flick of comprehension.

Pete, sweating, a trifle stern, opens negotiations abruptly. We turn our respectful attention to him (Salvatori wincing almost imperceptibly). We understand, Pete says, that he's the man to talk to about getting permission to swim in the Conte's pond, just over the field from our place.

The caretaker spreads his strong brown hands on the table and studies them. It is a complicated matter. He personally would have no objection, he says, except that fishermen pay the Conte to fish there. Obviously it would not do to have swimmers —

Pete says we wouldn't swim if anybody were fishing. The caretaker smiles and says that is fine; but naturally the Conte would not want to be held responsible if, say, there were a mishap. One needs protection against lawsuits, particularly a man in the Conte's position . . . Pete hastens to assure him we are both very strong swimmers. The caretaker listens, his gaze on Pete's face, frowning politely the way men do in serious negotiations. Feeling he's on solid ground and the battle's won, Pete leans back in his chair and tosses off the final drop of his grappa. Salvatori flicks his eyes to me. I give a slight nod — imperceptible, I hope, to Pete — and then drop my gaze modestly. I murmur that yes, we are both entirely competent swimmers . . .

Well then, the caretaker says briskly to Pete, he must get the Conte's formal permission, of course, but meanwhile if we are careful and do not disturb the fishermen . . . And Pete says masterfully that we appreciate his help, and they shake hands with great firmness, the way men do to indicate they have completely understood each other.

Staggering home along the dusty road with the grappa exploding in our brains and the sun laying flat the barley fields on either side and Peppina giggling uncontrollably between us, Pete brags about his triumph in a diplomatic encounter with a Tuscan peasant, who everybody knows is the hardest man in the world to negotiate with; and full of female admiration — *bravo, bravissimo, Pietro!* — magnanimously invites us both for a swim in his pond.

"When did you first . . . ?"
All lovers review the historic moment of apotheosis. He knows exactly: "When I first saw your face. At that reception, when I walked in and saw you standing there by the table, holding that glass and talking. Then you looked at me and asked me to get you some more vermouth and there was this click."
"Oh come now, Pete. Love is far too complicated —"
"I know that. Jesus, do I know that. But it has to begin somewhere, doesn't it? That click *was it, even if it was subconscious, too. In that little room behind the altar at the Medici Chapels, when you were showing me those crazy jars of bones. I never heard a woman laugh like that before. Right from the belly. It was so* carnal. *Standing there laughing carnal as hell in a roomful of bones. Jesus, the hair rose on my neck.* Pow."

"When did you first . . . ?"
"I don't know. I can't remember."
"You didn't want to know. I never saw anybody fight so hard against knowing something."

Removing traces of my occupancy of Pete's bed (hairpins from the table; slippers shucked on the rug; a long gray hair on the bottom sheet) before Gina comes to make it. Beside the book he's reading — Dickens's *Bleak House* — his wallet lies open. Snapshots in plastic billfold: group of four youngsters sitting on broad veranda steps; kid brothers and sisters. A tall man walking a stony beach with an Irish setter, hands in pockets, head bent, thoughtful: father. And a big handsome woman with a hawk nose smiling serenely over her shoulder from a lawn chair on a broad sweep of lawn, delphinium border behind: mother. I stare down into that matronly serenity for a long moment. Then slap the billfold closed. It lies on the table in a flat arch that duplicates the flat curve of his hip.

. . . Aaaaaahhhhhh . . .

and mingled with the sweat, the groan of ecstasy breaks open to salt desolation and a sob. He lies beside me and in the shuttered late-afternoon light his loins glisten, the sockets of his cheeks wash down a layer of glistening sorrows. Striking the center of his godhead he has broken through to the Little Death.

"So goddam little time. So goddam much to be done."

"What, love?" Sitting at his desk I look up from my journal. He lounges in the window of the bedroom, staring out over the valley as the sun squashes itself down between the breasts of the hills and the last light flames a sudden glory, bronzing his chest and face like a coin, a profile like Alexander's. Young Alexander, brooding in your tent: were there intimations of even your mortality? dead at thirty-three, with only the known world conquered? Oh unacceptable.

"There's so much to be done, and I haven't even started.

Do I have the right to be here?" The coin-profile, stern and bronze, ponders duty and sorrow.

And fear, with no warning cry, drops silent as a falcon out of the evening sky and plummets directly for my liver.

so another kind of instruction must commence. Was young Alexander sent out unequipped? Would Aristotle have dawdled in his instruction, schlupping peaches, mooning about the vegetable-patch, basking on thyme-scented banks, while his young charge grew sensuous and half-wild, scattering his vital energies in showers of golden coins?

I rise from the desk. Cradling my arms over my body I stalk slowly to the window. The last golden flush of the sky has vanished; the light deepens smoothly from green to kingly purple. Smoothly, I split open my gray silk robe; smoothly, silkily, I notch my breasts against his arm. The blond down stiffens under the tongueing nipple: the body's blind leap of ardor at the fuse, the automatic switch. And I tongue into him — tripping switches, fusing fuses — the old instruction: the matter of his value.

And afterward kneeling over him I wash the juices from his skin with a towel dampened in my mouth and I bend to kiss him reverentially, cupped between my prayerful palms. While the falcon pecks delicately at my liver, pausing to cock his head, listening.

Mrs. Beeton's Cookery Book

Kitchen Maxims:
— Clear as you go. Muddle makes more muddle.
— A stew boiled is a stew spoiled.

"What're you doing? Can't you sleep?" He staggers naked into the kitchen, blinking at me sitting naked at the table.

"Looking for a recipe for a custard, or something. These eggs are piling up so. And for some other way to fix zucchini, Aurelio keeps making me pick them . . . If Tim's been actually cooking from this book he's got the most exotic diet. Recipes for Pigs' Ears, Jugged Hare —"

"Is that what you do when you can't sleep? Get up in the middle of the night and sit around bareassed and read recipes for sows' ears?" He lumbers over and stands behind me and puts his hands over my breasts. "You're *pazza.*"

"It's sorta interesting. Listen to this: . . . *to prepare a suckling pig* . . ."

"Yeah, well, I know something a lot more interesting. C'mon, *pazza,* up."

". . . *first remove the eyeballs* . . ."

SCOOP. Folded tidily in the middle and hung over his arm like a waiter's towel I am courteously borne back to bed, where he has something very interesting to show me which he has no doubt is an entirely new concoction never before revealed in any cookbook, not even *Mrs. Beeton's.*

Goddam the fucken bloody
I drop the teakettle and run for the window. He's standing down in the garden, waist-high in beans, holding the edge of the hose from which issues nothing.

"Did you check the cistern?" I holler down.

"Hell yes I checked the cistern! I always check the cistern. It was full a couple of minutes ago —"

Down in the deep cave of the cellar: peering into the concrete vat, nothing but a dank mossy shimmer way below, a hollow drip drip. "I couldn't have used more than a few gallons," he grumps. He hates machinery.

"Tim says the pipeline goes through the bandits'. Maybe they'll know."

Peppina leans on her elbows out the window, contemplating the spit she's dropping down on the old hound curled in the courtyard dust. Spotting us she claps her hand over her mouth, melts back. One of her sisters-in-law appears; vaporizes, giggling. Vivarelli *père* appears. Grinning, calls out his *buona sera,* invites us up. We skirt the oxen twitching fly-swarms as they munch their evening hay, climb the stone steps to the inside door where the Vivarellis have lined up in formal welcome. Work our way down the reception line of eight handshakes, are ushered to the long table. The evening meal, a pot of soup, hangs ready over the fireplace; but ready too are *vin' santo* and *biscotti* and an assortment of company glasses. All set out waiting on the table. Pete and I exchange a glance.

There is some jockeying for position along the benches. Peppina is giggling so hard her oldest aunt gives her a jab with an elbow, hissing *zitti!* Peppina shuts up, barely. A pause — more pregnant than is formally required? — as we lift our glasses. Sixteen beady *banditti* eyes beading on us. *Saluti.* We drink. Bead-bead-bead go the eyes around the glasses, and the family grin threatens to choke them.

Two hours later, reeling back down the lane, skulls roaring and the first star jigging violently in the swinging eastern sky:

"Those bandits," says Pete thickly. "Can you believe shutting off our water and then trying to tell us it was accidental?"

"Accidental, they've probably been planning it for a week. What you have to understand, Love, is if they haven't got a TV what do they do for entertainment? Live off the land, of course." I wave my arm grandiosely. *"We* are the land. We are a natural resource, and *you* are the Grand Canyon—"

"Wanna know what I think? I think they think we're mother and son committing in — in —"

"— discretions."

We collapse in each others' arms and stagger home and try to commit same but pass out instead.

In the garden Aurelio and I confer. He stoops and picks up a clump of earth and palpates it in his palm as he talks. It crumbles out between his square fingers which are exactly the same color as the soil. *"Brava Signora.* You are watering the lettuces in the morning before the sun can suck out the juices." He compliments me in the manner of a kindergarten teacher. "This row of carrots is ready. These are too young yet, wait a week. The peas" — he snaps off a pod and pops it with a thumb, flicking them out like BBs — "are almost finished. You will pick the last batch tomorrow. But the zucchini must be taken or they will stop bearing." Squints at me severely. I look down at the zucchini which bask like baby alligators under their jungle of leaves. One would feed a family of five for a week. "But Aurelio, we have been eating them —" He stoops and with two blows of his machete, *zap zap,* severs two more. I totter up the steps, one tucked under each arm. Dump them on the kitchen table under the nose of Pete who is finishing *A Streetcar Named Desire* with his breakfast. "Oh boy," he remarks. "Zucchini for lunch and dinner again."

"Tell you what we could do. We could go out tonight after it's dark and dig a hole —"

"That's wasteful." Scandalized scowl.

"Yeah yeah," I sigh, "the starving Armenians."

"Armenians? Are the Armenians starving?" Ears prick, ready to get worked up over another set of helpless victims of somebody's imperialist greed (the topic of one of our recent seminars).

"It's just an expression. An old one." (Ask the Madonna of the Wallet, she'd remember it.) "So how do you want your zucchini today? Baked, fried —"

"Stuff it," he advises. "Yuk-yuk."

We have a kitty — "Kitty, for God's sake," he snorts; "what ridiculous names women have for things" — we have a kitty into which we put ten thousand lire each and when that's gone we put in some more. We use kitty money for all purchases of food. He handles the lire, I keep the books. He insists on going fifty-fifty with the supplies. "No woman's going to keep me," he says. "But Pete, I'm renting the place; you're my guest." "Listen, I may be a guest but I'm no gigolo," he says with finality.

I cheat on the books; I charge his side only a fraction. We eat mainly from the garden; marketing at Loro I hungrily eye the melons, the steak, the chickens but buy only the very cheapest necessities and great quantities of *pastasciutta* (spaghetti is filling). He notices nothing; he eats ravenously from his heaped plate; finishes the portion of cheese I press on him, saying I can't possibly . . . Men are so stupidly prideful. What will happen when he runs out of money?

He allows me Gina's wages but balks at my paying for his laundry. He washes out his own shorts and T-shirts and socks. His laundry is always dripping away in the bathroom or thrown over bushes outside to sun-dry. I offer to do it but he refuses. "I've been doing my own stuff for years at school. I can take care of myself just fine." "But that's silly, Pete. When you're married you'll let your wife do your laundry?" "That's different," he says.

— Man. Now that is *power*.
— What is?
— You. Sitting there on the edge of the bed brushing your hair. Pure power. Like one of those roomsize magnets. It fills the room.
— There is as much power in you. Standing there in the middle of my room.
— Me? Listen, I'm not talking about muscle power, I'm talking about
— I know what you're talking about. Just remember what I said, Pete. Men have that power too. Will you remember that, when you're standing in some other woman's bedroom?
— I can never imagine myself standing in some other woman's bedroom.
— You will. And when you do, you must remember that your power is as strong as hers.
— Jesus. It is? . . .

I'm getting in "condition," hard and lean (and hungry). We take arduous daily hikes, lengthening them. Back up dirt roads to hidden villages simmering in rocky vineyards and scrub pine, where dogs growl at us from the dust and old men follow us with mouths agape as we cross the wide spot in the road that serves as piazza. We are quite literally creatures from another world. The women doing their wash at the village pump fall silent, watching us, outlandish *fuorini* abroad like apparitions in the high heat. They do not smile; their faces are closed. They do not walk for pleasure.

Once, trudging back from a loop along the old road to Traiana, we spot a column of smoke. The late-afternoon sun is low and red against our eyes; we cannot be sure, but it is in the direction of

"The house!" Pete breaks into a sprint. I follow stumbling, lungs compressed with panic. In the distance a ridge of cypress dances like smoke pillars. The land is so dry; the fields and woods like tinder —

Around a bend, Aurelio's compound. He waves cheerfully as we draw up. He is leaning on his pitchfork, burning charcoal.

Wordlessly, Pete and I continue down the lane, climb the front stairs. The sense of deliverance is overwhelming. We stumble to the kitchen, lean against the table, gaze into each other's faces, overwhelmed with our deliverance.

There is a grace here. It floods us as we sit at the kitchen table in the morning sun. It inhabits the rooms shuttered against the afternoon heat. It seeps up from the arched dark chambers below, where have been stored the fruits of two

centuries' husbandry. It lies upon our shoulders as we sit, he
with a foot up and I leaning against his breast, in the broad
window of a summer's night, watching the fireflies ply the
sweet dark of the garden and the yellow moon rising to
wash the hills. It flows over our naked skins like the satiny
night air; it splashes in the windows as we lie on the bed, I
sighting down one leg propped on my raised knee, examin-
ing my foot making circles in the moonlight. Softly singing
lyrics from ancient musicals

> *Since I reached the charming age of puberty,*
> *And began to think of feminine curls,*
> *Like a show that's ty-pical-ly Shuberty*
> *I have always had a multitude of girls. . . .**

                              while lying beside me he lis-
tens attentively, like a child being told a story. I can feel his
listening, as we lie there, rocked gently in our hammock of
grace, suspended in this grace of disbelief.

"Madame. Bon soir. Permettez, je suis—"
The Conte of the Pond: most fashionable gent presenting
himself at the door during our unfashionably early supper
hour. Black silk turtleneck, via Veneto slacks; smooth dark
skin, silver temples and moustache. Polite eye smoothing
down my rumpled cords. To my response in French he says
in English, "Ah. Forgive. I understood the Signora was
French." Which disposes of my French accent, so I counter

* "Where Is the Life That Late I Led": words and music by Cole Porter.
Copyright © 1949. Reprinted by permission of the publisher, T. B. Harms
Company.

in Italian, which disposes of his English and we stand one-to-one.

The Conte (he assures me) deeply regrets interrupting my meal — I am holding a half-eaten raw carrot — but he merely wishes to assure himself I will not drown and (small elegant smile) sue him. We are very grateful (I say) for the use of the pond and we would not dream of suing him in the unlikely event we drowned. He has no doubt (he murmurs, smoothing my cords the other way) that the Signora is not only a competent but graceful swimmer. Does the Signora by any chance care for the pheasant shoot? He is shortly taking up residence at the Villa and if the Signora would care to join him and his guests he would be delighted to —

Pete has materialized in bulk behind me, in one hand a dill-sprinkled spear of raw zucchini. There are introductions (*piacere, piacere*). The Conte can see that the, uh, young man too can take care of himself nicely in the water and of course if he cares to join the shoot . . . pausing somewhat scant of formal delight. I say that unfortunately we will not be able to stay into the season. The Conte says it will be a loss to the entire countryside, and they can all only hope to look forward to the Signora's return; and *arrivederlà*.

Back at the table Pete says *Your* return, what about *my* return; and these Italian cats are all alike, so obvious, women are just sexual objects to them and he for one does not see how I could swallow all that hair oil.

I smile feeling nice and fat inside the way women do when lubricated with hair oil. I push the bowl of cherry-plums toward him and pour him some more wine. He ignores this and scowling puts his palm out on the table demanding mine. It waits while I leisurely select a plum, pop it into my mouth, savor the juices spurting against my palate; chew it a bit and then take the pit from my tongue and delicately lay it on his palm and close his fingers over it, one by one.

. . . *Aaaaaaahhhh* . . . Mid-afternoon, mid-siesta, and a crunch of gravel down in the courtyard, the sound of a car door slamming. We freeze. *Goddam the fucken* . . . I hasten into my caftan. The man comes up the steps tucking in his shirt the way men do in approach-patterns. *Buona sera Signora. C'è il professore* . . . ?

Americans. Travelworn little family — wife; child — on their way from Urbino to Florence stopping to deliver greetings and a bottle of arak to Tim, friend of friends (and hoping to exchange it for a few hours' respite, a drink, maybe even dinner?): nothing for it but to invite them in.

Simmons is the name, Gordon and Clare and little girl Sandy. He is smoothskinned with a curiously bisected beard like in the old pictures of Lucifer, associate professor of the Drama in some midwestern college. Clare is pretty; cool gray glance of a suburban matron, fine legs, broad hips. Both products of sound protein balance, Drivers' Ed., orthodontia, Dr. Spock. Young, in their early thirties. They accept my offer of a swim and dinner with such cool aplomb I am put on the defensive, as if it weren't quite enough. Pete slopes in, checks Clare's legs and Gordon's beard and introduces himself tersely: "I'm Pete Hatch." Declines to glance at me. Let them wonder; that's the name of the game, those are the orders.

We cut through the garden and the orchard (no comment on lush beauty of the land) and over the field to the pond. The bank of heat-crushed thyme, marvelously fragrant: no comment. The water, voluptuously, heavenly cool after such a long drive? No comment. The parents composedly submerge first themselves and then the child, and begin a swimming lesson. "Lie on your stomach, Sandy," the mother directs in her pleasantly modulated voice. The child, gasping, obeys. "Now kick," says the father in the same reasonable tones. They tow her slowly along, like a barge. The child submerges briefly, coughs, begins to thrash and grab. "You are not paying attention, Sandy," says the mother. (The temperature in that car must have hit the hundreds. Feeling on my own skin the fresh miracle of sensual pleasure I reflect that a few of life's joys may pass nice young Americans by, but none of the opportunities to educate their offspring.)

At supper I discover I've lost an earring. "It must have come out while you were swimming," Clare remarks. "I'm sure I would have noticed if you'd had only one earring when we came in." I wonder if she noticed I was covered only by my robe when they came in.

Midnight: still sitting around the table. After dinner Gordon rose, went out to the car, brought back a guitar and an enormous wrench for tuning it. This took a very long time. When he finally put the wrench aside and began to play there was no discernible difference. He wandered about from chord to chord, never staying long enough to enable us to detect a melody; he stopped frequently to correct the tuning, the fingering. I wouldn't mind singing along but with all these pauses there's nothing to do but sit and listen. He plucks meditatively, solemnly. After a couple of hours he seems to get the hang of it and plays a whole song through. "A whaling ballad," Clare informs us. He plays another. His wife sings along in a sweet true voice. They sing song after song I do not know. Pete doesn't seem to mind just listening; his is a generation of listeners. Pondering this is depressing; mine is a generation of panickers. I am trapped, claustrophobic. I squint out the window at the moon. I squeeze my eyes to make it look like two; tilt my head to line them up again. Try to ponder optics (Trachtenburg: was it during nine years of solitary confinement that he developed an entire new system of mathematics?) . . . Ballad after ballad plonks out of the guitar, stanza after stanza. Each is announced by Clare: "This is an Incan ballad. The melody is carried by conches." (A speed system, wasn't it, something to do with the magical quality of nines, you could take a whole line of numbers) Elizabethan ballads and Resistance ballads and Polynesian love ballads and Civil War ballads and railroad ballads and coalmine ballads and woodcutters' ballads and Polish, Thai, Somali, Iraqi, New Zealand folk ballads and a ballad of Gordon's own composition in Esperanto. The child, who has fallen into a fitful doze on the floor, awakens suddenly and begins to whimper. She wanders around the room whimpering and clutching herself. I suggest maybe she has to go to the bathroom, and offer to take her. "If she does, she'll verbalize it," says Clare pleasantly. "Play that medieval Sicilian one, Gordon." While Gordon plays the medieval Sicilian one the child nonverbalizes on Tim's Bokhara. "If you don't mind," Clare murmurs, "we don't react to communication blocks." I mop the carpet anyway, trying not to stigmatize any more than necessary. But the child flings herself on the musnud, bellowing. Clare finishes the last notes of a Moorish war ballad and continues in her pleasant voice, "Sandy. The people cannot hear the music. Do you think that is fair?" The child bellows louder, beats her feet, thrashes. I suggest that it is quite late and she must be very tired; perhaps a swallow of wine to relax her — "Oh no," Clare says, "no wine." I mumble something about how I understand American kids aren't usually given spirits but sometimes as a sedative — "Oh she has a little wine with water during meals once in a while," says Clare, "she is learning to taste everything so there won't be clandestine pressures and guilt associations when she's older. But we don't want it to be focused on as a dependency measure." "You mean," Pete remarks, "if she needs it that's when she can't have it." Clare smiles gently. Over the child's screams Gordon launches into what sounds like a Zulu initiation ballad. "This is a Zulu initiation ballad," announces Clare. One learns.

I excuse myself and in the bathroom spend a half-hour shaving my legs, straightening the cabinet, and rereading *The Waste Land*. A thump on the door: "Hey. You OK?" "No, cowardly. Is he still —" "Yeah. We've gone through the wine. You want me to get another bottle from the cellar?" "*No*. Hold the line for five more minutes."

I rummage through Tim's linen press and come out with a set of very holey sheets. Reappear to announce it is our bedtime. Here are sheets for the bed upstairs and there is also a bathroom there and I am afraid I am insomniac and sleep very lightly so I shall have to close all the doors between here and the downstairs bedroom wing. Never apologize, never explain: I retire. Leaving them in mid-ballad and to wonder if they care to why Pete disappears with me.

"Normal. You used to keep writing me about how I ought to settle down with a girl my own age and lead a normal life." Sitting in the bedroom window, gazing out at the setting moon. Telling each other that tomorrow they will be gone. But something has been broken into.

"*That's* normal." Pete jerks a thumb over his shoulder. "Out there, two normal Americans and a normal little kid. A decent respectable married couple, spacing their kids responsibly, bringing them up right, traveling a little, bombing the culture, ethnically aware — all that good normal stuff. Engaged. Enlightened. At home anywhere — my God, the Conte's pond might just as well have been the Country Club pool. Now you tell me this: is that what you've got in mind for me? Is that what I'm supposed to be learning and working for?"

I cannot answer. I can't put my finger on it: what is so repellent?

"Because if that's normal I don't want it. If that's what you mean when you talk about my great future, it is unacceptable." He turns me in toward his chest. He puts his face in my hair. "I don't want that and I can't have this. I can't hide here forever in this sealed-off Utopia."

The falcon bends diligently again to his task.

9 *summer*

"Hey."

"Wh."

"Listen." Stretched out on the Conte's bank of prickly thyme I am too exhausted from heat and hike to fall into the water. *He* has done his fifteen thousand laps around the pond, come to fling himself dripping beside me. "Hey."

"Ym."

"What do we pay for chicken at the butcher's?"

"Uh. 'Bout eight hundred."

"Eight hundred lire for a scrawny little chicken, and all these chickens running around the countryside! Whatever happened to the law of supply and demand?"

"Mff."

"There must be a hundred chickens pecking around the Vivarellis' yard, for instance. Whatta they do with 'em?"

"Sell eggs."

"Then how come eggs are so cheap and chickens are so expensive?"

I groan, flop over on my stomach, resettle my head in my arms. "Dunno. Go swimming." Close my eyes.

Presently: "Hey."

"Mmn."

"No swimming. At. This. Moment."

Open one eye to check out this tone. Open both. "Oh no."

"Oh yes."

Struggle up to my elbow. "No, Pete. Not outside."

Am batted down. "Yes. Outside. Yes." Am flipped over. Flash of white teeth in tanned face, grinning.

"No! Pete, I really mean it. Someone could see. Somebody could come over that hill — Pete, I don't want — I really don't *want* —"

He wants. Sundazed I stare up at him. He stares down. My eyes are pinned; arms pinned. Power-lock. Locked into his stare, a small cold burn of fury ignites in me. And sparks a cold blue click behind his retinas. Click of something being cocked. Staring into the cold blue is like staring up a gun-barrel. Focused dead-center on target.

"Damn you Pete you *can't*, I'm warning you *I won't* be —"

He can; I am. What I have taught his body it remembers; but I never stripped a face to tooth and bone.

— What, Love, all this lamentation over a little outdoor fucking? Pete, c'mon. I'm not mad anymore.

— A single second. In the space of a second a man could become a killer. At any given moment something can go *click* and a perfectly decent guy could turn into a killer, a rapist, an

—Really now, Pete, how can one's mistress, coy or otherwise, be raped? It was a

—assassin. Stop instructing me on this. It wasn't you felt
that click . . . That Arab, looking down the gunbarrel.
He

—but he was carrying the gun, Pete. He brought it with
him. Why would he have come with a gun if not with
intent to

—claimed afterward he loved Bobby. I could never understand that: how any guy could look straight into a living
man's face and pull the trigger. I understand it now. Oh
God I understand it now.

Painting: Peasants' Sunday Meal

Laid on the canvas with rich hearty oils: sepias, browns,
ruddy peasant flesh; the table a spilling still-life of fruits,
meats, blue cloth, bowls, pot of flaming geraniums. Rich
hearty variation of models: Aurelio at the center, short,
square, a block rounded only at the edges, neckless, ham-
mered to a redbrown singe by work and sun, eyes disappearing in an intelligent squint. Gina, a silent face, dignified,
skin a ruddy apricot, greenish in the shadows. The Nonna,
Aurelio's mother, strongly reminiscent of old Indian chiefs,
triangular profile, chin and nose a noble toothless pincer,
crop of stiff whiskers, traditionally gnarled hands. Aurelio's
son Mario, smelling strongly and inoffensively of sweat,
earth, oxen, a larger edition of his sire, simply shaped as a

baby, wearing shorts and sleeveless underwear top and a felt hat which is as much a part of him as his ears. Mario's wife Maria, bearing a remarkable resemblance to her in-laws, a no-nonsense girl of economical movements and words. And Aurelio's three-year-old granddaughter, a basketball of a baby, triumphantly confirming the endomorph strain. The muscle and energies around this table would power a locomotive.

Snitched by the artist from other men's canvases: a tanned blond giant from the Northern Epic School and a slight woman with a shawl of brown hair, from perhaps some comic strip (the Dragon Lady?).

Chicken broth with barley. Cold vegetables in vinegar. Cold sliced pork. Lettuce in oil with spikes of ham. Steaming chicken, garlanded with rosemary. Beet and onion salad. Nests of buttered parsleyed noodles. Towering *dolce* made of *biscotti* soaked in coffee and brandy and layers of chocolate and fondue of creamed sugar-eggyolk-butter. *Vin' santo*. Chianti. Grappa

"Eat," urges Nonna, jabbing me with her elbow, "you're skinny as a pitchfork. Hee hee hee." Aurelio fills and refills our glasses with chianti. Over my protests he says *"Puro, sano, non fa male. Sincero."* Pure, healthful, won't poison you like sophisticated city food. What one does not oneself grow is forever under suspicion: insincere.

Mario goes over to a large cage in the corner in which are three very young larks, or thrushes, infant speckles still on their breasts. He takes them one by one into his huge hand, crams a piece of chopped meat into each bill, dips each into a glass of water, tips it up to make the water go down the throats. The birds feed eagerly and then, set back in the cage, squinch down and close their eyes. Mario picks one up again and brings it to me; but I demur, smiling. "It is too young," I say. "Young creatures are very tough," says Mario, but he puts the bird gently back into the cage. They will be released when they're old enough to fend, he says.

Huge storerooms full of black hanging hams and sausages and salamis, clusters of raisins drying on racks, casks of ripening wine, vats of olives and salt pork; stone silos to be filled with maize; hogs fattening in pens beneath the cypress grove; honey-hive humming in the vegetable garden; hutches of rabbits, pens of pheasant, quail, ducks, geese, chickens

Carrying his grandchild against his chest Aurelio proudly shows us the fruits of his labor and his wisdom, the cornucopia of his husbandry. *Sincero.*

Staggering back up the lane in the twilight, Pete calls for Diocletian reforms. "Why can't we live like that? Why can't everybody live like that?"

"Because we have fallen from the Garden."

And to prove it we make love, eating from the fruit of the knowledge tree till we're stuffed purely full. Nature's bounty run amok.

Mrs. Beeton's Cookery Book

4 pigs' ears	essence of anchovy
breadcrumbs	egg
veal	butter size of walnut
suet	gill brown sauce
parsley	fresh ground pepper

Hunched at the kitchen table over my reading, he over his: *War and Peace.*

— Pheasant croquettes. Gooseberry pudding. Ox cheeks? Beet curry . . . Pete? D'you suppose curried zucchini with hard-boiled eggs?

— Sounds fine, fine . . . Jesus, I'd forgotten the feel of this. The great epic passion, y'know? He's got the excitement of it.

— Mmmhm. I wonder if it'd be too mushy

— Those fantastic battles. I remember reading it when I was a kid. Submerged in it for days. It really turned me on, made me burn with excitement, you know? I mean I used to be able to understand it.

— Understand what?

— War. What makes a man want to go where the action is. I couldn't wait to grow up and be a general.

What will I do when he notices I've not asked him for this week's kitty contribution? What will he do when he notices he has only six thousand lire left?

Suddenly wakened in the night; my own screaming wakens me. Arms scoop me powerfully. *What is it? Baby, tell me what is it?* Gasping wordlessly I indicate. He seizes my calf and massages it gently between his palms. "Only a charley horse," he says after it's gone abruptly as it came. "Jesus. I thought you were being murdered or something." His face is pale with sweat in the moonlight. He holds me against his naked chest and rocks me. Rocks us both, like babies.

Dear Mrs. Hatch,

I have it on reliable source that your son Peter, who has been visiting in Italy, is preparing shortly to return to the U.S. where he plans to battle sin, poverty, war, prejudice, corruption, stupidity, inequity, pollution, police brutality, imperialism, arms proliferation, wiretapping, materialism, suppression, neofascism, and other social ills. This is all very well, and far be it from me to deny that things need to be done both at home and abroad. But I feel that Peter is far too valuable a man to risk in such dangerous, not to mention thankless, activities. Men who attempt to force change on societies are apt to wind up either incarcerated or assassinated.

It seems to me that Peter would be more valuable to society in the long run if, instead of risking his neck, he would just settle down with a nice girl and pass his fine New England genes down to some fine New England sons, who might then go out into the world as a team, thus greatly increasing the power to get things done — and attenuating the chances of tragedy, as it would take an assassin too much time to keep reloading.

Think it over, Mrs. Hatch. If this makes sense to you — and it will, if you value your son — you must do everything in your power to persuade Peter, on his return, of the common sense of settling down with a nice girl right away; and perhaps making a career out of teaching, which would seed his intellectual and moral ideals in the young, thus passing on and continuing the line of high genetic virtues.

I am sure, among the daughters of your friends there in Boston, there must be a number of young women of good birth and rockbound upbringing who would consider themselves honored to become Mrs. Peter Hatch.

— A Friend

He's got the whole world
In his ungh *hands*
He's got the whole wide world
In his ungh *hands*

Floating up from the hillside, where he is digging out the collapsed entry to an old root cellar as a present to Tim: the uneven baritone, surprisingly pure. Broken only by an occasional crack (even from the vegetable patch I can see down into the baby's assailable skull) and rhythmic grunts as he heaves boulders.

He's got the little bitty babies
In his ungh *hands*
He's got the little bitty babies
In his ungh *hands*
He's got the little bitty babies
In his ungh *hands*
He's got the whole world
In his hands.

Never (Mama said) tell a man bad news on an empty stomach.

I wait until after breakfast to inform him the refrigerator's sogging up. "Hell, no problem," he snorts. "Kerosene's probably low." Carefully follows Tim's instructions to remove and refill the reservoir. Tidily takes the glass to the sink to wash it. Neatly cracks it in two.

"Lord. Why didn't somebody tell me you couldn't put hot

glass under cold water?" moans our Future Leader, looking at me accusingly.

Bugs: thrashing through the boscage of the hillside canyon I swat swarms of midges, horseflies, mosquitos, buggerish blackberry vines. A picnic, he has decided, would be nice. Marvelous it is how gentle green alder and bracken brush at *his* legs (nice: brown and elegant and blond-downed, swinging on ahead of me) while in his very footsteps nettles and thorns claw at *mine*. I turn to swat at a horsefly biting my calf and discover we're being followed: two black puppies. *"Via!"* I shoo. Pete turns. The pups sit down in the grass, tongues lolling. *"Via!* Go home," I command. The pups eye me warily, hopefully, unmoving.

"Aw." Pete surveys them. The pups get up, wagging tails, ducking heads respectfully. Pete holds out a hand; they wriggle toward it. "Pete, don't encourage them. They'll be all over us and the picnic—" He has a palm under each ecstatic head, scratching. "Pete—" "It's OK," he decides, giving the heads a fatherly pat and turning uphill again, "they're nice little guys." "But we won't be able to get rid—" "C'mon," he commands. The puppies plunge after him.

They watch politely as we eat our picnic. "Don't feed them," I warn, "they'll follow—" He has divided the cheese-crust in two; they take it courteously from his hand. "They won't eat it, just chew on it," he says. The male pup has one black ear that stands up straight and one white that flops. The female is sweetfaced, timid. She takes her cheese-crust a polite distance off and gnaws a moment, then tires and puts her head in her paws, watching. "She looks kinda thin, poor little fella," says Pete and divides the rest of the cheese between them.

They follow us down the hill. At the road we try to shoo them gently back. "Stay," Pete commands; "go on home now." Three times we cross the road. They follow. A Fiat squeals wildly around the bend. "Pete!—" He makes a rescuing tackle. No use: we carry them across the road to safety. They trot home at our heels. We put them in the car and drive back up the hill-road. We let them out close to where we figure they found us. "They'll find their way home from here," says Pete. "But I don't see any houses around," I say. "Dogs can always find their way home," he says. We set them chasing after a bone and take off fast in the car. A half-hour later the pups appear on the front steps.

. . . *"Abbandonati,"* says Aurelio next morning. The pups have established themselves under the steps, with their water and food dishes ("They gotta have water," said Pete, "we can't let an animal go thirsty"; and — before bedtime — "We can't let an animal go hungry"; and — in the middle of the night — "It's their instinct to bark, protecting the property. Quit worrying. We'll find out who they belong to and take them back in the morning."). *"Abbandonati,"* Aurelio says firmly, explaining that if they belonged to somebody they would have licenses, in this area which is a game-preserve all dogs are licensed and of course kept tied up, if they run around loose they will be shot on sight by the game warden or the *contadini,* stray dogs are a menace; and he recounts the story of a stray who in one night killed twenty chickens. Here they are not like the Florentines (Aurelio says) who keep useless poodles, feed them like children at great expense. He hoists his pitchfork and goes off down the lane, pausing to make a rather elaborate check on the ducks in the pond. The puppies loll on their haunches, gazing adoringly up at Pete. They are appealing, I admit to myself. All young things are appealing.

. . . "The thing is *we* can't keep them," I say at supper, after a day spent in the car driving from farmhouse to farmhouse. "It wouldn't be fair to them, taking them in and then having to leave — They can't come inside, they'd chew up Tim's rugs and things, and have you noticed how everybody in the neighborhood keeps mentioning those twenty chickens, and then having to put them in the car when we take a walk, the road's so dangerous — and unless we keep them tied up all the time —"

"No. That's no way to treat an animal, keeping them tied up day and night." He scowls, hunkers down to scratch the worshipful heads. "Goddam little nuisances," he mutters. They lick his face.

. . . "The thing is farmers just don't consider dogs pets," I say as we trudge back from Loro, where we have gone to consult the local *carabinieri* (*Lost* dogs? the Captain said in amusement; these are perhaps hunting-dogs? We said No, just mongrels — "but very sweet," I found myself saying, "*carini,* one has a lop-ear —" "*Molto intelligente,*" said Pete, and the Captain smiled the way people do when they don't understand you at all; and Pete, beginning to sweat, said maybe the Captain might know of a family who would like a pair of puppies for their children; and the Captain smiled and excused himself to answer the telephone, and his aide, grinning widely, showed us out the door). "It's natural I suppose, farmers have a different attitude about animals,

they have to earn their keep, all the dogs you see tied up to
the barns are hunting-dogs, even Aurelio's. . . ."

. . . No, Aurelio says, these are definitely not hunting-
dogs. Besides he does not need another. Hoisting the male
pup up by its unmatched ears Aurelio patiently points out
the ways in which it (dangling in his grasp) is not a hunting-
dog. "OK, OK," winces Pete, hauling the pup back into his
supporting palm. It licks his chin. Pete looks at me over the
furry lop-ear. His eyes are bleak. "It's my goddam fault," he
says, "I took the responsibility." "It's nobody's fault." I reach
down to pick up the thin little female. "They would have
followed us anyway. It's the dog's instinct to attach themselves to Man. Their nature isn't your fault." "It's my responsibility," he says starkly.

. . . "The thing is there's nothing else to *do*," I say as we
drive to the *veterinario's,* the pups frolicking excitedly in
the back seat. *"Niente da fare,"* shrugs the vet, a beefy man
with a cigarette dangling from a holder at the corner of his
mouth; these *cani abbandonati,* they cause accidents on the
road, they may become rabid, they kill chickens, they are
shot and sometimes they die and sometimes they are only
wounded; *niente da fare. Una cosa tragica, Signora,* he adds
urbanely around the cigarette, noticing my face. Pete's is
pale under the tan. "Look. We want to know," he says
tightly, "how you do it." The vet does not understand. "How
you kill them," Pete says; "we want to know how it's done."
Aah, the vet says; a pistol.

"But I thought an injection! At home they just give them
an injection!" I scrabble at the sleeve of Pete's T-shirt. "Tell
him a pistol's too noisy, he'll shoot one and the other'll be
terrified, it won't do, it won't do at all, tell him he has to

give them an injection, my God, he's a vet, he ought to know how to handle animals without terrifying them —"

"The Signora says a pistol is not humane." Pete keeps his regard on the vet. "She says an injection. Can you give them an injection." The vet removes his cigarette and says something very fast and smoothly ending with Bam Bam. "What's he saying, Pete, I can't understand what he's saying —" "He says a pistol is humane." "Oh but the noise! Tell him —" "Never mind." "But —" "Never mind, I said. Just — go back out to the car, will you. Wait outside." "But tell him —" "I'll tell him. Go wait in the car, I said."

. . . He sits in the bedroom window. The last rays of the sun cut his profile against the applegreen sky. He sits motionless, staring out at the fields as the golden light drains, evening slowly settles. Down over the Val d'Arno a gentle mist turns silvery. From the lane below the orchard a cry floats up, *Buoi! Arrgh! Buoi!* as a Vivarelli urges his oxen home.

. . . *Aaaaahhhhh* . . .

". . . Pete?"

"Mnmnmnmn"

"Do you know my first name?"

"Mnnh — Huh?"

"What's my first name?"

"Your first . . . Now that is a strange question to ask at this particular moment. Do I know your first name. Jesus."

"But do you?"

"You know something? You're crazy. Asking me a question like that at this — Listen, is that what you were thinking just now? While we were —"

"Do you realize you have never once called me by my first name? Not once."

"Jesus. H. Christ. Do women *think* while they're making love? My God that is appalling. That's like having three people in on it. One of them watching. Jesus. Whattayou think about? The state of the world? Recipes?"

"I think about why you don't ever use my first name."

"Women. It's scary, you know that?"

"You think it's not scary wondering why?"

"Why what?"

"If you've been raised the way I was, never to call an older person by his first name."

— Marry me.

— Oooh I'd love to but there's this congenital insanity in my family, skips every other generation

— Listen, I mean it. I'm asking you to marry me.

— Now darling you don't want children with a third eye in the middle of their forehead, do you? Sometimes that happens in miscegenetic matches. Think how the poor kids'd be discriminated against.

— Miscegeny. That's what you mean, isn't it. The difference in our ages would make it like miscegenation.

— Yassuh.

— Why can't they let people alone? How's it hurting them? Two people who love

— Gotta protect the purity of our gene pool, sonny. Keep it purged of unnatural

— Quit calling me sonny. You're back on that old crap again, about how I should lead a normal life with a young wife who'll give me a dozen kids

—Make it eleven. With your genes, think of the football team you could field

—Listen. Can you imagine what genes you and I could pool?

—How do you want your zucchini today? I can bake it, sauté it

—We were talking about having kids. I'll want them eventually, when I've got a start on my work. When I do I want them to be yours.

—By the time you're into all that work, sonny

—God damn it, I said quit calling me sonny

—I'll be long out of your life. How long do you think it's going to take you to save the world? How long do you think I can have babies? How long

—Don't cry! Jesus don't cry again, please don't

—do you think we have? How long do you think the world has?

—How did we get into this again? Oh baby please . . . Here, wipe your face

—I'll wipe it if you'll look at it. Will you look at it and try to see it? Damn you Pete, *look!* Look at the age in it, look at the craziness, look at the fatuity and the blindness and the

—Oh Jesus God I can't stand it. Don't you know I see your face? Don't you know I see its age? Don't you realize I see it and I love it? Listen, age is a property of your face, like those gray eyes and that sad mouth and the way it's beautiful. And yeah, I see the blind look too sometimes. But I'm not blind. D'you think I don't recognize what I see? D'you think I don't know what I love? D'you think I'm so goddam young I can't understand what I love?

—too late, too late, everything's too late

— D'you think it's easy to be young? Carrying around all
this load of love, all the years I gotta keep lugging it
around and without you there's nowhere to rest it
— too late
— with you turning your face away from me, the only face
I will ever love like this. No other face will ever look like
yours to me, and you keep turning it away

Sunday morning, and I am out of cigarettes. Trudging to
Loro (olives dripping silver in the cool morning light;
eddies of cool and damp rising in the grassy ditches by the
road) he grumps: "I can't understand it. A strongwilled
woman like you walking eight kilometers for a few tubesful
of tobacco."

Two A.M. It's coming. I can smell it. The storm that's
been threatening all day approaches, rumbling in the distance over the valley. I lie drenched from dark dreams and
his sweat, which healthily combats the muggy night even
as he sleeps. His young body moves in a snug insulation all
its own; the heat breaks through my brittler defenses. I
rise and prowl naked through the rooms, uneasy as an animal. Finally hole up at the central place, the kitchen table,
with *A Streetcar Named Desire*.

His gaze, so recently traveled over them, has left a spoor
which sweetens the pages. ("Blanche may have been a linthead," he decided, "but she was tough-fibered. She hung in
as long as she could.") I never had much patience with
Blanche — poor blasted creature, rent fragments of silly
bellehood safety-pinned like rotted silk underwear over the
grime of loneliness and aging — but with his charitable

sweetening, in the yellow light of this kitchen bulb and this superheated night, Blanche's agony takes on authority.

Whoever you are — I have always depended on the kindness of strangers . . .

The storm edges closer, crackling like teeth. An airless weight compresses my chest and sucks out oxygen; it settles between my shoulderblades and breasts, clings to my belly and thighs and hips like a wet winding sheet.

Now, honey. Now, love. Now, now, love . . .

CRAAAAACK the sky overhead splits open, cracking every rooftile in half and lighting up the room in a flare so phosphorescent that everything, stove shelves pots sink crocks kettles baskets winebottles, at a single instant burns into my retinas a black-and-white negative room.

I am seized with a bone-chill that rattles my chair. The flash comes again; the camera lens gapes wide. I shelter my head in my arms.

CRAAAACK the sky rips again and under the hammer-blow I hear the chink of tiles raining from the roof. I feel the first trickle of the leak, like the first chill freshet of air, against my nape and shoulders. Time will begin to leak in through the chinks and soon, very soon it will be —

CRAAACK. Tinkle, tinkle of rooftiles. Tinkle, tinkle like little drops of time, raining in. Soon it will swell to a flood and I will be washed away.

Head sheltering inside my arms I weep.

"What're you — Hey. You scared? Or . . . Oh baby. Baby baby baby." He shelters me, rocking. "Baby ah come on now. Hey. Come on, come on. It's OK, you don't need to be scared, I'm here . . . Ah baby please don't. Quit that now, it's OK, I'm here." Rocking, sheltering.

Morning: a lemony calm. He says, "I never had you figured for the type to be so scared of a thunderstorm."

I mumble something about the roof falling in.

"That roof's hundreds of years old. It'll be here long after we're gone. Funny, I didn't know you were really scared of anything. You're always so sassy."

"Another idol crumbled." What do I have going for me but sassiness?

"No, it was kind of . . . beautiful. Your being so scared, I mean. You felt so small when I put my arms around you, so . . . naked and sorta, you know, unprotected. Even more naked than you feel when we — I don't know. It touched me. Jesus, I felt *fatherly*."

Later, apropos nothing but the muggy silence: "Listen. You never have to be scared when I'm around. You remember that. OK?"

The day continues baleful and oppressive. I awaken from my nap feeling as if I'd spent it pinned under something large and heavy, say a Victorian chifferobe. Sky colorless as pewter, humid, bloated. Teatime is listless; bread and honey too thick and sweet. He suggests we go back to bed. We try that awhile but our skins feel like that plastic they use on dolls now — lifelike but inert, incapable of combining chemically. He says maybe what we need is exercise. I protest: how could I walk five hundred yards in this heat? We'll swim then, he decides. Hauls me up and bullies me into my black bikini.

. . . Down the lane through heat-flattened grasses. At the bend, the old apple tree where on the first morning of Creation I picked hard green little apples and carried them back and cut myself and filled his belly full of little green apples and a seedlet of my blood.

The pond is flat and colorless. It is like swimming through mercury. We haul ourselves out and the water clings to our bodies like chain-mail. Go clanking back up hill and in the courtyard an old man is dismounting from a rickety bicycle. Bringing Pete a cable dated yesterday.

His Stern and Rockbound
DRAFT BOARD
Requests the Presence
of
MR PETER HATCH
at
A HEARING
In His Honor
in
Boston, Massachusetts
USA

September Sixteenth
Nineteen Hundred and Sixty-Eight
Anno Domini

La Napoule France Tuesday 5:32 p.m.

We arose at 7:32 a.m. and breakfasted in our room. We walked around the village, which is small and pleasant, far nicer than Cannes would have been although he said he'd like to take a look at the Beautiful People before they vanished from the face of the earth. His money has run out however so he insists on staying here where it is cheap. He is forced to borrow from me although his is not a borrowing tribe. We went to the beach at noon and returned to the pensione at 5:10 p.m. and now he is napping before dinnertime

I am the keeper of the Books and Minutes. I sit at the little table in my gray robe transcribing History from the lines in my palm, reading off data from memory banks and making double entries in the ledger. My script is spidery, Spencerian. I pause occasionally, tapping tooth with pen, to squint at him sprawled asleep on the bed. Turn and with a judicious flourish make more entries, underlining firmly here and there.

His arms and legs and chest are badly sunburned. We were 5.4 hours on the beach today, and here on the Mediterranean the fierce old sun is tough on young people; the air is thin from overuse and the sun roars more fiercely as the season's end approaches.

I am the Historian, he is History. He fuses and drives it, stages and mounts the production; he is planning a cast of millions. The Historian makes prophecies. "You will win," she predicts; "you will overcome. You will hold the whole world in your hands. You will lead your people out of Egypt."

He eyes her uneasily. It is he, not she, who is to be responsible for all this. He feels the perilous vulnerability of his sunburned skin, the brief blaze of his powers, the burden of his youth and love and other gifts.

But who would argue with the Historian? With the Life Force? With predictions, which are always self-fulfilling?

He had a theory that the Mediterranean's salts, washed into the basin over eon's of occupancy, compose a sort of nutrient broth like amniotic fluid whose specific gravity is exactly that of the blood's. It was, therefore, he felt, impossible for him to sink in it. He did seem marvelously buoyant; his big body floated light as a barge before loading. He spent 3.5 hours swimming and the other 1.9 lying beside me on the beach. I sat trying to read but the sand got in my book and my hair and eyes and between my toes. My muscles ached with the isometrics of irritation. I bundled myself in towels to keep out the sand. He thought that because he had a tan he would not burn; but where his skin was sheltered over his loins it was a milky, almost bluish white. My skin simply turned darker and thicker.

Daily as we traveled he washed out his socks. Everywhere we lodged they hung from basins and bidets, on doorknobs, over the railings of bedsteads and balconies.

We departed with gifts: from the Berninis, two huge bottles of Aurelio's puro e sano *chianti; and Peppina brought over an enormous basket of hard little unripe apples.*

The last dawn approaches. I will braid my hair tidily, pin it up off my neck like Ann Boleyn. I will put on my summer dress. I'll have them bring up strong black coffee and strong-crusted bread and we'll breakfast out on the balcony in the strengthening sun.

Before dinner on the last night we sat on the balcony of our room drinking the chianti and lobbing apples down through the plane trees below, under whose canopy the tables were being set for supper. We heard thumpings, astonished curses from the waiters. At eight o'clock we marched down to dine. Seating us at our table the waiter apologized for the spotted cloth. "Une pluie mystérieuse," he explained. Perhaps the gods were playing tricks, he said, shrugging with his mouth the way the French do.

The strong new light will blaze full in my face. He will look into it and transcribe History from its lines; from its spidery Spencerian script he will invent beginnings.

After dinner we strolled down through the village and gazed through the gates of the Saracen fortress, its stony face still guarding the shore. We sat on the stone abutment bordering the promenade and watched shadows stroke the beach clean of the day's litter.

And now it is morning and the moonpath has gone from the water and everything is blue and golden in the lifting sun. Our belongings are packed and stacked near the door.

We sat on the balcony and watched the moon rise. We sat watching the moon rise over the Saracen fortress, and drank the last of the Tuscan chianti.

I sit here in my caftan making final entries. Soon I will rise, and cross to him sleeping on the bed, and touch his shoulder. He will rise like the sun and go forth.

He groaned in his sleep. The sunburn gave off such heat, like the sun itself. He groaned as he held me, a groan like a sigh. Propped on my elbow I watched the sleep streaming like a comet's tail across his face.

I close the ledger. I go to touch his shoulder. He rises, shedding flakes of skin and sunlight.

The green grass grows all around. At the toy Cannes airport the green grass grows all around the pretty little flowerbeds with their bitty little poppies and big stiff zinnias. He is getting a grass stain on the seat of his jeans. What will the Bostonians say to that? "They'll want to know if I got fed on the plane," he decides. That would be the Madonna of the Wallet. She would give thought, as mothers do, to his belly. He growls, "I better get fed, goddammit, with the price I paid for this ticket."

I have paid for the ticket. And I have loaned him 20 francs, which is all I've got left until I can get to American Express. A man has to have something besides his wand to wave in his pocket. Even if it is French francs, which he suspects is Mickey Mouse money although he has observed me transform it with *my* wand, my ballpoint pen, from real American dollars and real Italian lire. He is into me for over $100 but he is a Boston man and no gigolo and he will pay me back. I may be 250 years old by the time he clears the slate but it will, by heaven, penny by penny, be cleared. Meanwhile I can survive on the interest.

He spits green grass and speculates up at the blue Mediterranean sky into which he will be launched like a stone from David's sling in exactly

"What time now?"

"Seven after."

twenty-three minutes. He stares at his wristwatch. Astonishment slowly refills the sockets of his face. Recently he has been forced into one-to-one confrontations with clocks, calendars, lunar and meteorological storms, biological tides. He has not yet determined if History is a metered continuum of microflows or something he can afford to snub. To him time has become sidereal. Who can understand twenty-three minutes? "Damn," he mutters. Crushes his knuckles into the grass.

"Come on. I'll buy you a coffee." I rise, brush grass from my skirt with a slow wiggle of my fanny. Astonishment drains, leaving a puddle or two of grief. We have deepened those sockets where it lies, he and I. "You're such a carnal woman." He says this for the last time in the same *eureka!* tones in which he announced it for the first.

"Infinite variety resides in the eye of the beholder," I say, polishing the last little apple of instruction.

Slowly we cross the grass, his letter-sweater with the crimson block H flapping like a pennant in the breeze. I lag and watch him lope away from me.

In the barred shadow of the airport gates he turns. It's his spin, last turn to shoot the sun, take a final fix on the position. I stalk slowly toward him, swaying my hips for a bit of a twinkle. When the weather turns cold, and it will, it will, there should be something for him to twine verdantly still around the dear ruin.

"You look beautiful in a summer dress," he says.

Inside, boardings are announced for Paris, Genève, *les*

États-Unis. At the coffee bar he says to the girl, *"Deux cafés,"* and to me, *"I'll* get it." Reaching authoritatively into his jeans for a couple of my francs.

"Thank you," I say.

"My pleasure," he says.

10 *fall*

"What I need," says Arabella to the Cabin Steward, "is a waterproof jacket."

"A jacket, Madame? Waterproof?" He fingers her gray silk robe with his eyes, the way the French do (*since the sixteenth century,* she notes, the way archivists do, *when they checkmated the Florentines by appropriating the silk industry*). "Ah; Madame means the life jacket? It is stored here, at the top of Madame's closet—" and the Steward opens the closet from which tumble a number of notebooks and papers. He stoops stiffly but she directs him to leave them be. He drags the bright orange life jacket, its straps dangling like broken limbs, from the shelf and lays it on her bunk. "*Voilà,* Madame," he pants, "although it is not likely that Madame will find need of flotage equipment. This ship has been certified by the French Government and the Maritime Commission to be unsinkable." He permits himself a patriotic French smile. "There is, of course, a Lifeboat Drill in which all passengers are required to participate. It will occur immediately after tea. The instructions are posted on the back of your door — *ici* — in four languages. At the sound of the alarm bell you will don your jacket, fastening the straps as illustrated, and proceed to your designated station on the Boat Deck. It is, of course, a formality only. There will be demonstrated the raising and lowering — *Pardon,* Madame?"

"I said if there's something gone wrong here, you can tell me. I won't panic," she says dryly.

"Pardon?"

"Never mind. What I want is a waterproof jacket," and she taps a large ledger lying on her desk, "for this. Something to wrap it in so it won't get soaked and sink. Something to keep it dry and afloat." She adds crisply, "It's valuable. Irreplaceable, you understand. Wouldn't do to have it sink."

"Sink, Madame?" The Steward has begun to look liverish. He spreads his liver-spotted hands (*old hands,* she notes; *the Steward is older than he'd first seemed*). "Valuable, Madame? All valuables may be given to the Purser for safe-keeping. May I suggest —"

"Fat lot of good it'd do locked in the Purser's safe at the bottom of the ocean, now would it," she says reasonably. "The idea, M'sieur, is to keep it afloat. Surely you can find me something . . . ?"

"We cannot be responsible for valuables left in the passengers' cabins, Madame," says the Steward, beginning to whimper the way old men do. "The Purser —"

"Please. We may no longer care much about ourselves, you and I," and she smiles, wheedlingly; "but it is our duty to protect records, for the future." He totters out, quavering that he will try, Madame.

At a table: Arabella and an ancient French Prioress. *"Finis coronat opus,"* says the Prioress, grasping the wine decanter with a hand so old it looks like a falcon's claw, "My life's work, just completed, is a tapestry depicting the Descent from the Cross. There are peacocks in the folds of the Magdalene's robe. The tapestry measures thirteen by twenty-one meters. The dried blood of the stigmata is rendered in droplets of applied garnets." The Prioress's trembling grip splashes red wine on the white cloth. "The Holy Ghost is revealed, *in puris naturalibus,* as a female."

"Right on," murmurs Arabella. *"Ars longa.* Why is everybody on this ship so old?"

"All is relative, *ma fille.*" The Prioress slowly hoists her glass. The cloth around her plate is stained like a battlefield with wine and bits of torn flesh. She drinks and eats and her skin sinks farther back against her falcon's cuticle-skull. *"Dum spiro, spero."*

She is jarred awake by a sudden silence. The engines have stopped. The stillness chimes in her bones. *It's coming:* Chill sweat erupts between her breasts. She lies staring into the black. She waits. The stillness deepens to a muffled beat which is the intensity of silence.

Presently she rises, throws on her robe, pads barefoot out of her cabin. On deck the sultry stillness condenses, takes on presence, a massive thickening of air and water. There — out there, beyond the thinner stretch of black — the Dark

Continent: Africa. The drumming silence gathers power. The huge night drums with its soundless pulse.

She struggles back to her cabin and it is like swimming through tar. Kneeling on her bunk she pushes the curtains back from her porthole. A far faint spiral of lights, climbing a great black cone: Gibraltar.

She pulls the curtains closed. Without taking off her robe she lies down again, arranging herself in the prescribed position on her back, arms folded over her bosom. She waits.

It comes: the engines lurch, the huge screws churn, the ship hangs shuddering; then with one great bucking lunge it clears the straits. Squeezed out from the warm old womb of the Mediterranean into the icy Atlantic.

In the morning the decks are glazed with ice. At noon a stinging sleet comes to lash the promenades. By teatime they have entered a dense white fog which seems, patterning itself against the windows of the salon, to be composed of snow crystals.

"It's too early for this," she protests to the Cabin Steward as returning to her room she finds him turning back her bed, "it's still fall, not winter. We must be far to the north of our course. Or is the Captain trying to take us over the Pole, like an airplane?"

"Madame need not concern herself with the ship's route." The Steward smiles urbanely. "It has been plotted electronically, for the safest and most comfortable passage. Rest assured, Madame, you are in competent hands."

"Old hands," she says dryly. "Tell me, how long have you been in the employ of the Line?"

"Fifty years, Madame. Since I was an adventurous boy of nineteen. A mere farm boy from the Limousin —"

"Don't you ever feel it's time to retire? Return to your, er, peaceful pastures? Pack your mementos and take your gold watch —"

"*Moi, Madame? Jamais.*" He tilts his Steward's cap over one eye rakishly, the way Maurice Chevalier used to do. He makes a chipper little shrug with his feet. "What need have I — for whom time means little, Madame — of a gold watch? *Moi — jamais.*" He winks, gives the bed a pat, and totters out.

Even the *memento mori* (she notes) of a gold watch cannot dislodge the old. It is the young who drift the world like ghosts, looking in vain for a place to materialize; ghostly stowaways on old, doomed *Titanics*.

It hits at dinnertime. The ship slams into the first great tsunami, driven before the blizzard; there is a crack and a paroxysmal shudder and they are lifted, suspended; then with another shattering crack and a crash of glass and silver they slam into the trough. "An iceberg!" an old gent screams; "we've 'ad it, mates!" The ship wallows violently, shakes itself like a terrier, begins its upward heave. "Ship's time is 20:30," bongs an old whitebeard, "latitude 6-8-point-6 degrees North, longitude 3-nought-point-4 degrees East, barometer at 29.77 and falling!" "Goodbye, Dad," cries an old lady to her husband, "it's been swell. Through all the years and all the tears it's been just swell, hasn't it Dad?"

"*Quem Deus vult perdere, prius dementat,*" observes the Prioress, with the back of one claw slowly sweeping aside the broken glass littering her battlefield, and with the other picking up her fork.

"*Carpemus diem,*" Arabella murmurs setting glasses upright and pouring them both some more wine.

Four days and nights the blizzard rages. The great screws shriek, the ship shudders and heaves; its prow batters through sheet after sheet of wind and water frozen in solid panes like safety glass; spray after spray of shattered ice crashes against its hull and upon its decks. Tinkle, tinkle. Ropes are strung along the walls of corridors and salons; like mountaineers clinging to the sheer faces of cliffs the passengers cling to ropes as they struggle their way along, calling to one another. Above the howl of the storm and the gnash of the ship's agonized timbers their calls are chipper, doughty, convivial. "We're 'angin in, we bloody well are," cries the Cockney gent to Whitebeard as they lurch past each other on their hands and knees, each with an elbow hooked over the corridor ropes. "Ship's time 16:30 on the nose," Whitebeard booms out. "Latitude 5-9-point-nought degrees *UFF* North and longitude 4-2-point-6 degrees East. Cape Farewell off the starboard bow!"

Arabella entertains herself with the phenomenon of the weightless staircase; timing her descent with the crest of the toss and the ship's shuddering pause before the plunge she floats down in that old sweet dream of levitation. Coming back up, to keep herself in condition, she toils against the upward heave, hauling 2 Gs and 220 pounds. Sometimes, to balance out the natural order of things, she goes down the down staircase and up the up.

Still hanging in on the fourth night, the storm and the Captain's Gala go on as scheduled. *"Bis dat qui cito dat,"* the Prioress murmurs, noting the bottles of festive champagne set out in chrome tubs bolted to the tables. *"Facile princeps,"* Arabella agrees.

The old waiter lurches over and pops the corks and fills their tumblers, which like the rest of the table service are fitted in slots to prevent tumbling. The Prioress closes her talons around her glass and slowly hoists it. *"Fiat justitia, ruat coelum,"* she proposes. The ship swoops down. A column of bubbly coils up out of the glass like a waterspout. She directs it neatly into her beak.

"Oh my, Dad, I don't know if I should," the old lady titters, "what if it makes me giddy?" "Drink up, Mother, and we'll go out and spoon at the moon." "Oh Dad, you know there isn't any moon tonight," she giggles. "It's out there somewhere, Mother. Somewhere up there above all this dark and stormy night that old moon's still up there ridin high, Mother, and don't you forget it," the old gent wheezes, "lightin the road to love, hee hee hee."

Mimi,
My funny little
Good-for-nothing
Mimi —
Am I the guy?

A youthful spot of color high on each old cheekbone the Cabin Steward struts his chevalric stuff under the rosy spotlight. Twirling his cane jauntily, clinging to its support now and then as his knees buckle, he belts out his number; his thin old bleat fades and strengthens as the spotlight totters after him, losing him once in a while; cap pushed over one eye, dentures flashing rakishly, he shuffles his way through four bouncy choruses before he gives out, sinks to his knees, waves his cap high in an expiring bleat, and receives gales of applause, *huzza! bis!* The Crew Talent Show is a geriatric triumph.

The orchestra sweeps into the *Blue Danube Waltz*, the Ballroom floor fills with dancers. A fine popping of kneecaps and champagne corks mixes festively with the strains of the waltz and the groan of the timbers and the shriek of the gale; rotating disks cast shifting spots of color over jewels flashing on raddled old bosoms and dangling from long, long ears; nostalgic scents rise of *muguet de bois,* old ladies bridle and neigh as they totter about in the gallant embrace of old gents whose wattles are tucked tidily into high starched collars and crisp white ties. "Damn the torpedos," quavers one as he twirls slowly past, "full speed ahead!"

"Right on," murmurs Arabella. Somebody taps her shoulder. She turns. A tall spare old gentleman, dressed all in white, requests the pleasure of a dance. "Right on, Captain," she says.

"Cognac?"
"Thank you."

"May I say that is a very pretty dress, Madame?"

"Thank you." Erect on the Captain's sittingroom sofa Arabella smiles correctly. "It's a summer dress."

"Perhaps that is why it is so becoming. Madame has the look of summer still lingering."

"Pretty long linger," murmurs Arabella, "given this untimely season."

"We will be out of it tomorrow," the Captain says. Despite the weariness in his voice, it is authoritative. "How grateful one is," Arabella says in tones that are far harsher than she intends, for she truly is grateful, "to be told what is going to occur tomorrow, by somebody who seems to know."

"Experto crede?" The Captain permits himself a spare, weary smile. He folds his long frame stiffly into a leather chair.

"You've been talking to the Prioress."

"She is my aunt."

"What a coincidence."

"History is composed of coincidence, Madame. I understand you are a Historian?"

"I used to be. I found it too full of coincidence."

"My aunt tells me you are also a teacher. Or have you retired also from that?"

"Historians and teachers never really retire," she says wryly, twisting her mouth the way people do who feel the prick of an old sliver, "they just become archivists."

"And where are your archives, Madame?" The Captain crosses his legs, lifting one knee over the other with his hand.

"At a University in the Midwest. I've accepted an appointment there as Curator of Collections." Sharply, because the sliver has moved into the region of her liver, she adds "I don't really know why, except that it struck me as the logical place for things to be collected — the Heartland."

"I am not sure I know Madame's meaning," the Captain murmurs; "as a seafaring man I am not overfamiliar with matters of politics and terrestrial geography. More cognac?"

"Thank you." The Captain's eyes must once have been blue, very blue; but now they have bleached to the gray of a winter ocean. Arabella blurts, "I thought you'd be young."

"Pardon?"

"I mean I'd come to imagine that you'd be a quite young man. I felt a . . . valor, a sort of determination, guiding the ship. A toughness of will — and, I suspected" — she laughs, not too defiantly — "a lack of directional sense. All of which I usually associate with the young."

"You admire the young, Madame?"

"Some of them."

"Then I am complimented. Although I'm sure that the sense of, ah, valor emanates in most part from the passengers, Madame, yourself included. As for the ship's course, I must submit that it was God who guided the storm toward — You are pale, Madame. You are unwell? Shall I ring for the —"

"No. I'm fine. A bit tired. It's been a pretty exciting Gala," and she smiles politely.

"Valor is tiring?" He too smiles politely.

"I'm sick of valor. I'm sick," she continues, folding her fists tidily in her lap, "of hanging in. I'm sick of Romanticism, Captain, which is a balingwire operation. Held together with balingwire and it's got to be invented as you go along and every day you have to get up and invent another way to keep everything wired together," she says with a brilliant smile, "because yesterday's wiring's come loose. You keep hanging in, Captain, and you find yourself hung up at the end of a balingwire noose."

The Captain stiffly unfolds his tall old frame, places a palm on each arm of his chair, stands. He stands over her, polite, infinitely weary, waiting for her to leave, the way Captains must, so he can tend to his final duties of the night. "Metaphor is beyond me, Madame. I am a plain, seafaring man."

"It's not metaphor and it's plain enough," she says, composing herself. "I've been away from my country a very long time." But she rises, smiling extends her hand to him. He bows stiffly over it.

"*Merci,*" she says.

"*Mon plaisir,*" he says.

At four o'clock in the morning, four days late, the ship slips silently past the point and into the river's mouth. The night is tepid and utterly still. Arabella is alone on the forward deck, leaning on the rail. The water glides like oil under the ship's keel as it moves slowly upstream. Arabella senses, as a pressure against her skin, the gradual thickening into mass of the great city's bony towers; she feels, as a preliminary quiver against her eardrums, the soundless throb of the continent.